ODDS

'N

ENDS

This is a work of fiction. Names, characters, places, and incidents either are the product of the author's imagination or are used fictitiously, and any resemblance to actual persons living or dead, events, or locales is entirely coincidental.

Copyright © 2016 Roy L Cover

Publisher: Cover Publishing

ISBN: 978-0-9982021-0-5

Contents

To my dearest friend *Becky*,
whose inspiration and support makes my writing possible,
and *Anita* who turned that writing into a book.

A HUNTIN' WE WILL GO

My vacation was half over and I had already accomplished most of what I had planned to do, which was mainly sit around and do absolutely nothing. So in a fit of boredom I called my neighbor, Frank. He's an avid hunter. I haven't hunted anything since fifth grade when some older guys talked me into going on a snipe hunt. I didn't see a single snipe all night, or one since. That pretty much dulled my interest in the sport. Still, I admire people who challenge nature's most dangerous beasts with nothing more than sheer guts, and whatever killing merchandise the sports emporium sells.

As luck would have it, Frank was about to set out on a short hunting trip and invited me along. The present boredom sharpened my dulled hunting interest, so I threw on an old sweatshirt, blue jeans, and a pair of running shoes. I had never run in the shoes, but figured they could get me away from any hungry creature with me on its menu.

I went out the back door and saw my wife kneeling in her garden. She looked up from under her wide brimmed straw hat and asked, "Oh, come out to help?"

"No. I'm going hunting with Frank."

"Hunting what?"

"Whatever he hunts, I guess."

1

"Where did you get a gun?"

"Nowhere. I'm not really going to hunt anything. Just going along."

She stared at me a moment in silence before turning her attention back to her garden. An unwary weed caught her eye and she ripped it out of the ground and threw it aside. "Well, don't expect me to clean or cook anything you bring back."

With her implied permission and encouragement, I headed over to Frank's house. I'd never been inside, but I always imagined how he probably sits in a big leather chair with his feet on a tiger skin rug, while he admires his trophies of exotic animal parts on the walls. Probably smokes a pipe and sips cognac.

But I had to be content with my imagination. I saw him standing next to a workbench in his open garage when I walked up. He was dressed from head to toe in camouflage clothes, floppy hat, and black and green paint smeared all over his face. I could just barely see him.

He looked me up and down and spit a stream of tobacco juice into an empty beer can. "You're not goin' dressed like that, are you?"

I looked down at my outfit. "Did I miss something?"

"The only thing missin' is the conductor of your brass band. You couldn't sneak up on a deaf and blind turtle in that outfit."

"We're going to hunt turtles today?"

He raised his eyebrows. "You hunt turtles?"

I gave a little laugh. "The only things I hunt for are my car keys or the remote."

"You're puttin' me on, right?"

"No," I answered. "That's pretty much the extent of my prey."

After I told him about my snipe hunt experience, he turned around.

It sounded like he was coughing while rummaging around the top of the bench.

After several moments he faced me again. "Well, we're not going snipe huntin'. But first we have to get you into some proper duds." He bent down and took the lid off a small barrel next to the bench, pulled out a camouflage shirt, and tossed it to me. "Put this on. I wore it a couple times, but it should be okay."

I pulled off my sweatshirt and replaced it with his camo. The sleeves fell past my fingertips and it hung almost to my knees. It smelled like a sweaty bear suit had been wrapped around a dead rat.

He followed up the shirt with a pair of camo pants. The pants had the about the same odor as the shirt, if the dead rat had been exchanged for a chunk of Limburger cheese. They almost fit as long as I held them up with one hand, but they could have been about a foot-or-so shorter.

"Now you're startin' to look ready to hunt," he said as he tossed me a length of twine.

I used the twine to tie around the pants, then rolled up the legs a couple dozen times. It felt like I had fallen into a pile of rejected rags behind a Goodwill store.

Frank was replacing his snuff with a new lip-full, but stopped halfway and frowned when he saw my white shoes peeking out from within the folds of the camo pants. "Guess we can just rub some grass on those when we get out in the field."

My wife had given me those shoes last Christmas in hopes they might encourage me to run off a few excess pounds. Grass stains on them would probably upset her more than anything I could possibly bring home to clean and cook. Or for her to watch as I cleaned and cooked the thing myself. "You think," I ventured, "I could just go

3

barefoot and rub some grass on my feet instead?"

"We can use grass on 'em out there, or a can of green spray paint here."

"I'll wait for the grass."

"Good 'nuff."

I began the job of rolling up the shirt sleeves. "What are we going to hunt, anyway?"

"Dove."

"Not," I chuckled, "the dove of peace, I hope."

He looked at me like I had just suggested we do the tango in his driveway.

"Just a little joke, Frank."

"Yeah." He nodded. "That's about as little as a joke can get."

"Is all this camouflage really needed to hide from a dove?"

"Not from the birds. But you can never tell what else you might run across. Gotta be prepared."

I went to work rolling up the other sleeve. "You mean like a rabbit jumping out or something?"

He finished buckling up a shoulder holster and drew out a Dirty Harry pistol. "It'd better not."

When my eyes shrank back to their normal size I said, "That would take care of any snake, too, huh?"

"Naw," he answered and pulled a knife the size of a sword out of his boot and waved it under my nose. "Use this for snakes."

"Wow," I said in all sincerity, "You're just like the cowboys in the Old West."

That produced a huge smile as he picked up a compass from the bench and put it in his pocket. "Yep. Gotta know the land."

"I don't mean to be picky, Frank, but didn't folks in the old days

4

just look at the moss on trees for directions?"

"Sure, but there ain't always a tree around."

"Couldn't you just get on your hands and knees and look at the moss on the grass?"

He stared at me a moment as if I had invited him for another tango. "Moss don't grow on grass. Besides, who wants grass stains on their camos?"

"But they already have green on them."

"Yeah, but in all the right places." He gave me a look as if to say, *I dare you to say something to that.*

I decided to change the subject to something he would more readily relate to. "What's your favorite gun, Frank?"

His mood instantly brightened. "Just a sec. I'll show you." He walked over to a large double-door safe against the wall and stood between it and me while he worked the combination.

With the doors open I saw enough weaponry to overthrow a fair sized banana republic. He carefully removed a long gun and turned around, but didn't offer to let me hold it. "This here's an antique Frontier sixteen gauge. Mint condition."

"Wow, sounds like enough gauges to bring down a 747."

Frank picked up a rag and carefully wiped off the Frontier before returning it to the safe. "No, the smaller the shotgun gauge the bigger it is." He pointed at a gun beside it. "That's a twelve gauge. See how much bigger?"

I nodded without understanding a bit of it. "That gun above it must be about a fifty gauge, huh?"

He showed remarkable patience with me. But then, he was talking about some of his favorite things. "That's a lever action thirty-thirty, but it's a rifle. Rifles come in calibers. The bigger the caliber, the bigger shell it shoots."

"Uh huh," I said with absolutely no more understanding than I was about the shotguns. "You think that thirty-thirty could take down a dove?"

That made him hesitate a bit, but he recovered after a couple seconds. "It can drop a deer, I guess it could bring down a dove if you could hit it on the wing. Shotgun's what you use for dove."

"Oh," I said with my consistent lack of understanding. "I didn't know you had to shoot them in the wing."

His recovery time increased two fold. "No. . .you see, a rifle only shoots one bullet at a time. But a shotgun shoots out a whole bunch of pellets."

"Oh." I didn't even bother to add 'I see,' since it must have been fairly obvious by then I didn't.

Frank decided to play offence awhile. "You have a favorite gun?"

"Well, not really. I had a BB gun as a kid I liked, but I haven't seen it since I got married."

He spit into his beer can. "Then I take it you ain't gotta a gun for huntin'?"

"Oh, no. I don't have a gun for anything. You see my wife—"

"Yeah. I get it."

"I thought I'd just go along and keep you company."

"Uh huh," he said with about the same enthusiasm as if he was about to join me in that tango.

"I could even carry your gun for you until we found a dove if you want."

He leaned back against the bench in silence for several moments before taking a deep breath and saying, "Tell you what, sport. It's gettin' a little late to be going out today. I gotta better idea."

After listening, I said, "That's a great idea, Frank!" I quickly changed clothes and raced back home.

My wife was standing at the kitchen sink washing some of her garden fresh lettuce when I walked in. She immediately wrinkled her nose and demanded, "What on earth have you been rolling in?"

I hadn't noticed the camo's smell had rubbed off on me. "Just some hunting odor, dear. Guess what?"

The wrinkling of her nose was persistent. "Tell me after you take a bath."

"Okay," I said as I hurried off to the bathroom. Over my shoulder I added, "Frank is going to take me snipe hunting tonight."

End

DEAD FRED

I lead a quiet and simple life. I'm respectful, honest, and rarely drink anything stronger than an occasional sherry. Yet here I am in a hospital bed with bruises from head to toe, a monster hangover, and a police detective who has just read off a long list of charges against me that could not possibly have been my fault. They include assault, destruction of private property, disturbing the peace, hit and run, public intoxication, slander, and brawling. Although I'm sure the last charge should have read *bawling*.

Yesterday the office was being remodeled, which provided me with a day off. I decided to fill the tank in my cherished little import, and simply lounge about in the park, or even take a trip to the zoo in the way of some excitement.

I gently brought my temperamental car to life and carefully entered traffic toward my favorite gas station. Before I reached the posted speed limit, however, a funeral procession overtook me on its way into the R.I.P. Cemetery. Out of respect, I pulled over to the curb and waited for it to pass and enter through the gate a half block ahead. My respect quickly turned to curiosity.

I watched in amazement as dozens of pickups and larger trucks in the procession growled or wheezed past. Each one hauled ladders, shovels, tools with electrical cords, small machines with little motors on them, and pieces of equipment I couldn't even guess what their use might be.

There were commercial vans from every imaginable building trade, and every now and then a well-worn station wagon filled with undefinable objects or people in work clothes rattled past. No washed or polished sedan in the bunch.

Midway through the long procession, my amazement blossomed into burning curiosity when a white van with four huge loudspeakers mounted on its roof cruised by. As it turned into the cemetery the speakers came to life and shook the ground with Johnny Paycheck's old country song, *Take This Job and Shove It!*

It was more than I could take. I simply had to see what this bizarre funeral was all about. A gap between vehicles allowed me to coax my old import into the procession behind what had to be a landscape company van with the hand-painted letters, *Mary & Jane Grass Service*.

I followed the *Mary & Jane* van to a spot on the far side of the huge crowd forming in the middle of the cemetery. A much smaller crowd instantly formed around the van the instant it stopped. I thought it rather odd to conduct business at a funeral, but oddity appeared to be the norm here.

I left my car intending to ask someone about the affair and be on my way. But before I took more than three steps, a dented pickup slid to a stop within an inch of my left foot.

The driver revved the engine twice before turning it off and tumbled out with a six-pack of beer in his hand. He wore dusty jeans, stained plaid shirt, and brown work boots. I suspected he may have had a beer or two before he arrived by the way he stumbled into his own pickup.

"Long live the *BACOCWA*, brother," he said, weaved over to me and shoved a can of beer in my hand.

Without thinking where I was, I amiably answered, "Cheers," and took a sip of the beer.

It was obviously the correct response, because he nodded, drained his own beer, and reeled off to the left. I sipped on the beer while I thought about my next move. I wasn't sure now whether to ask someone about the affair, or a *BACOCWA*.

The small knot of men gathered next to *Mary & Jane's* van were heavy smokers, and I do have my allergies. Instead, I decided to walk toward the center of the cemetery. I didn't want to intrude at the grave site itself, but I was sure to come across somebody along the way who could clear up these little mysteries.

Before I had a chance to clear up one mystery, another one presented itself. As I walked along I saw picnic ice chests, buckets, tubs—even metal barrels—filled with ice and cans of beer. A small group, mostly men, gathered around each container and everyone held a beer. I also saw large buttons, like campaign buttons, pinned on several shirts, but they were too far away to read.

Practically the entire cemetery now held small groups around various containers, while another group congregated at the center, which I assumed was the grave site.

It seemed logical to me the more outlying groups would be my best choice for information, since they would probably be less intimate with the recently departed. Striking up a conversation with a stranger was difficult since those loudspeakers still shook the ground over and over with Johnny's song. And most people stood close to each other and engaged in their own conversations.

I continued to wander and take in the spectacle when I nearly knocked over a young lady. As I apologized, I saw she sported one of the large buttons on her bulging blouse. The word *BACOCWA* was printed in bold white letters on a red background with a number of small words around the edge. I tried to make out the fine print, but her heaving chest made it difficult to make it out.

Several moments passed before I became aware of the man standing beside me. Like the young lady he also wore one of the buttons, only his had been forged into a belt buckle—which was approximately eye level to me. The fine print quickly came into focus, *Benevolent Association of Carpenters and Other Construction Workers of America.*

I let it all sink in for an instant. The drunk's words came back to me, so I leaned my head back and shouted over Johnny's song, "Long live *BACOCWA*, brother."

It was hard to tell if he rumbled back with "Cheers," or "Beers." My attention had been drawn to my left shoulder when he sent a giant hand down on it in a show of camaraderie. My shoulder felt like it was dislocated.

His lady friend came up with a can of beer for each of us, which I accepted with my good arm. I popped the top, took a rather healthy drink, gamely croaked out, "Cheers," and eased off in another direction.

Before I had gone more than a few yards, a skinny man wearing a yellow cap with the word *CAT* on it rounded a large tombstone directly in front of me. The sudden encounter took us both by surprise and the collision sent him sprawling to the ground.

He had somehow managed to hold onto his beer, but his cap had been knocked off. He sat up and stared at it through bleary eyes. My own beer had gone sailing off somewhere and I bent over to pick up his cap for him. As a way of apology I said, "Long live *BACOCWA*, brother."

"Cheers," he blurted, and smartly jerked his can of beer up to drink to the battle cry.

I was about to grab his cap when the edge of his beer can clipped me on the chin as it shot upwards. Fortunately, I'm not a heavy bleeder, and the throb in my shoulder disappeared the instant my teeth slammed together and put a notch in my tongue.

In spite of the pain it caused when I talked, or maybe to take my mind off it, I asked the drunk as he regained his feet, "Who was the deceased?"

"Somebody die?" he slurred in a loud voice.

A guy in a blue and white polka dot cap passing nearby answered, "Fred's dead."

The bleary stare of my dangerous comrade took on a mournful look as he blubbered out louder and louder, "Oh no. Not Fred. Not ol' Fred Gunther?"

A familiar rumbling voice drowned out Johnny, "YEAH. WHATCHA WANT?"

The drunk shouted out, "Fred, Fred, you're alive! Somebody told me you died."

"WHO TOLD YOU A DUMB THING LIKE THAT?"

With the giant Fred Gunther's question ringing in my ears I watched the drunk's expression change from grief, to elation, to confusion as he tried mightily to sort things out. He finally seemed to come to the conclusion I had played a dirty trick on him about Fred's death. His expression took on a darker mood.

I didn't think an explanation of my innocence in this little misunderstanding had much chance to penetrate his inebriated state. It probably wasn't important anyway, so before he could fully focus on me I eased off in yet another direction.

Chance encounters weren't working out too well, but I was more determined than ever to find out what this whole thing was about. All the groups I had seen so far were somewhat rowdy with a lot of loud laughing and backslapping. That last beer had made my tongue somewhat numb, but I didn't think the backslapping would do my shoulder any good. I decided to keep walking until I came across a more laid-back bunch.

A few minutes later I spotted three men and a raven-haired, blue-eyed beauty calmly standing around a small ice chest. There wasn't any backslapping and their conversation was barely loud enough to be heard above Johnny's song, which *still* thundered through the air.

I hung back until the elbow bending brought a beer to each mouth of the group at the same time before I stepped up and casually asked, "Sure was a shame about Old Fred, huh?"

The temptress lowered her beer first and gazed across the little circle at me, while the tip of her tongue slowly licked across her even white teeth. A wedding band gleamed on her finger. She breathed a sultry, "I'm Gloria."

"Fred who?" asked the scruffy bean pole standing beside me.

"The Fred that's dead," I answered without thinking.

The squat redhead of the bunch had a good natured look behind his bushy mustache and proved to be as helpful as he was friendly. "Must be Fred Oakum. Only other Fred I know is Fred Gunther. But I think he's still around."

"Oh, yes," I quickly replied. "Old Gunther is still around." That bit of information gave me a slight sense of belonging.

"You know Gunther?" The suspicious question came from the burly bear sporting a tangled beard and wearing a battered hardhat.

"I'm Gloria," the sexy-somebody's-wife offered again.

"Well, uh, through a friend." I was beginning to get an uneasy feeling.

Red pitched me a beer. "Any friend of Ol' Gunther's a friend of mine. You know the Fred that's dead?"

"Uh. . .not very well." I fumbled with the can, popped the top, and took a large drink.

"Damn sure ain't no union man," the bear growled. "You must be a relative."

"Distant. On my mother's side." I took another large drink. The temperature seemed to be rising all around me.

"I'm Gloria."

"Damned relatives like a bunch of cockroaches. Come outta the woodwork soon's a man's dead."

The temperature kept climbing. I drained my beer.

I was ready to place my empty can with the rest of the empties crumpled in a pile next to the ice chest when Red tossed his own empty down and fished out two full ones. He pitched one to me and belched. "I'm gonna go find Ol' Gunther."

It was my chance to bring the temperature back down. "I'll go with you. Think I saw him over there a few minutes ago." I gestured with my head in the opposite direction of where Ol' Gunther had been.

Before Red caught up with me I had covered over six yards and drank half my beer. "Hey, you goin' to a fire?"

His question planted a strong suggestion in my mind. "No, but I'm beginning to feel like I could put one out."

He laughed and slapped me on my left shoulder. "C'mon with me. Men go behind that Herschel tombstone. Girls use the Winston stone over there. We get the tall one 'cause they gotta squat anyway."

I laughed along with him, even though his slap had brought back the throb in my shoulder. Some things are simply more important than others.

After we had left the hospitality of the Herschels, I felt better and asked Red, "Is there someplace I can chip in for the beer?"

"Naw. Comes outta the Union Funeral Fund along with the rest of the stuff. Plenty for ever'body."

"You mean there's more things than beer?"

"Oh sure. Union's got ever'thing those fancy cop funerals got. You know, big show of support here at the cemetery and all. Even gotta honor guard."

"So," I mused, Fred died while building America. How poetic." The beer was doing its job on me.

"Not exactly. I think he got shot by a jealous husband. That kinda thing happens a lot. Don't matter none. Long's the dues are paid up."

"But how does the beer fit in?"

"Simple. Union's got a lotta members." Then he winked and added, "Lotta jealous husbands, too."

As we walked past a barrel of ice and beer, Red grabbed two cans and handed me one. "Folks get tired of goin' to funerals. 'Specially when they don't even know the guy that's dead. Union Funeral Committee came up with the idea of giving ever'body a day off with pay and all the beer they can drink if they make a good showin' at the sendoff. Makes the union stronger."

It was all starting to fall into place. "Then the song that keeps playing over and over must have been Fred's favorite?"

"Probably not. We use it for all the funerals. Kinda fitting, huh?"

I thought about it while taking another healthy drink and listening to the words. "You know, you're right. Especially the part, '. . .I don't work here no more.'"

"Now you got it!" Red laughed and took a swing aimed at my left shoulder.

I was too quick for him this time. His hand swooped through empty air as I ducked and nimbly sidestepped to the right. But before I could congratulate myself on this unaccustomed dexterity, I savagely barked my shin against a low marble tombstone and lost my balance.

My forward momentum sent me stumbling and falling headfirst into the middle of another small group of drinkers. Luckily, my fall was somewhat broken when my elbow cracked against the edge of a washtub of beer and ice.

Before the world stopped spinning, a mass of muscle clad in jeans and a sleeveless T-shirt stepped up and clamped a powerful hand onto my left wrist. Like a magician whips a tablecloth out from under a set of dishes, he yanked me to my feet.

"C'mon, sport!" said Hercules. "No layin' down on the job when we got all this beer to drink."

I saw Red out of the corner of my eye walking away, no doubt in search of Ol' Gunther again. Hercules shoved a beer into my hand and gave me a hearty slap on my left shoulder. "Drink up, sport."

My left shoulder pounded, my shin felt like it was cracked, my elbow was on fire, and I suspected a mild whiplash. At least my tongue didn't hurt as long as I didn't talk.

I was silently whimpering into my beer when I felt a gentle tug on my pants leg. Glancing down I saw a cute little girl in a frilly dress smiling up at me. She was about four years old, and there was something vaguely familiar about her big blue eyes.

"My little girl," beamed the brown-eyed Hercules. "I'm babysittin' her this morning."

He looked down and said, "Hey, Cissy, why don't you give the nice man here one of your buttons?"

"Okay," she piped up in a tiny voice, and ran to a cardboard box several feet away. I had no idea what she was going to do, but the little pixie had a plan.

She pulled out one of the giant *BACOCWA* buttons from the box and held it like a dinner plate above her head. I could see the button's spike-like needle gleam in the sunlight as she ran back toward me as fast as her little legs could carry her.

Instead of slowing down to a walk as she neared, she leaped into the air and made a slam-dunk with the button—evidently in an attempt to pin the thing on my chest.

The button's point landed near my armpit the same time her little sharp-edged shoes slammed against my tender shin and scraped down to my instep. Since she held onto the button, the needle ripped its way down my left side until the point lodged firmly in my fourth rib.

"Ain't she the cutest thing you ever saw?" Hercules asked, as if he was actually proud of fathering such a hellcat.

My breath was coming in short gasps through clenched teeth, but I managed to screw my grimace into a fair smile imitation in spite of the pain. "Thank you, honey," I hissed.

Her evil smirk faded as she turned away from me. "Daddy, I gots to go to the Winston again."

"I knew this was gonna happen soon as your mother wandered off." Hercules took a deep breath and out-bellowed Johnny, "Gloria! Come and get your kid."

I decided I had seen enough. I began limping off in the direction of my car. My wanderings had taken me to the far side of the cemetery, and what seemed like hours of painful trudging, I found myself at the grave site.

"Shhh," came from someone behind me. "The service is almost over."

That's when I noticed how quiet things had gotten. Even Johnny had quit braying, but I had been unconsciously mumbling my own version of his song. I stopped and looked over at the casket resting above the open grave.

Directly across from me was what had to be the honor guard. Seven carpenters stood on line in full regalia of striped bib overalls, loaded tools belts, and a big yellow pencil tucked behind the right ear of each man.

They solemnly stood in their most professional workmanlike stance. Each man wore an aloof look with one thumb hooked casually onto the bib of his baggy overalls, and a mug of steaming coffee in the free hand.

In measured unison they shifted their weight from one foot to the other, and the only sound in the still air was the soft clunk of tools in creaking leather belts. And the occasional slurp of hot coffee.

Even in my discomfort, I was caught up in the mournful moment. I tried to show some respect and stood a little straighter as an eighth carpenter sauntered up to the honor guard and gave the quiet command, "Getcher staple guns out, boys."

Not even a muffled cough broke the silence as seven gleaming, chrome plated staple guns were brandished and loaded. The entire cemetery seemed to hold its breath.

Then, in a reverent tone, the order was given. "Nail it."

BAM! BAM! BAM! Twenty-one staples sailed through the still air in tribute to a fallen comrade.

I was simply overcome by it all and openly cried without shame. One of the staples was embedded in my right eyelid.

The silence continued for several more seconds until a beer popped open somewhere. Then another. And another. Soon it sounded like a string of firecrackers had been set off as dozens of cans snapped and popped, and Johnny once more told the whole world what it could do with his job.

I hobbled off toward my car again. Along the way I saw the hearse, limo, and some of the other vehicles pull out of the cemetery. It looked as if the climax to the affair was over.

Several groups were still clustered around some of the larger tubs and barrels, but as the beer thinned out, so did the people.

I could just make out the top of *Mary & Jane's* van when I heard a familiar voice off to my right. "Hey, sport. Still got some beer left. C'mon over."

"No thanks," I yelled back. "I've got a hot date waiting for me."

I lied. His little assassin was back with him.

I could now see my car through the thinning crowd. It looked like a long lost friend. I turned and took a last look at the fading carnival-like atmosphere. It had been an experience I would not soon forget.

Not far enough away for comfort at another barrel stood the giant Fred Gunther and his girlfriend, Red, the bear in the battered hardhat, and the falling-down drunk.

Somehow the drunk recognized me. He pulled on Gunther's arm and pointed at me. I could make out only a few of his words above Johnny's song, "Fred. . .that's. . .tellin'. . .you're dead."

The giant stared across the couple dozen yards separating us, while the drunk continued to babble and the burly bear added his own comments and gestures. I couldn't make out what was being said, but their conversation attracted others, including the Hercules. From the looks of things, none of it was in my best interest.

Like looking at a train wreck, I couldn't help but watch while Fred's stare grew dark and ominous, and the others caught the mood. I tried an apologetic smile, but it didn't go over too well. With all my pain it probably looked more like a sneer.

Before I could think of a way to make a graceful exit, Gunther crumpled his beer can in a huge hand and headed my way. It looked like the friendly encounters were over.

The distance between us rapidly disappeared with his long powerful strides, and the others were right behind him.

My reserve strength kicked in. *Sheer panic.* I ignored my pain-wracked body and made a mad dash to my car and jumped in.

The key bent in the ignition as I frantically twisted it against the START position. It broke off just as one of the four cylinders made a feeble cough and struggled for life.

I wildly pumped the gas pedal and yelled out the name of every saint I'd ever heard. I promised God, my mother, and Johnny Paycheck I'd spend the rest of my life in a monastery if I got out of this mess.

What seemed like hours, the other three cylinders sputtered to life and I savagely rammed the pedal to the floor and held it there. I had visions of my precious car being wadded up like an empty beer can and tossed into Dead Fred's grave—with me in it.

The rpms built up.

The tachometer trembled in the red, and Johnny was completely drowned out as I jammed the gearshift into first and popped the clutch.

I thought I heard the crunch of glass and shouts behind me as I streaked past *Mary & Jane's* van and careened off a tombstone, but I laughed hysterically and didn't look back.

But the hysteria and panic failed me as I slowly coasted through the cemetery gate and saw the fuel gauge calmly resting on EMPTY. But I didn't look back—not even when I heard a beer can pop open in the back seat and heard that sultry voice, "I'm Gloria."

End

Bops

There comes a time in many of our lives when it becomes necessary to call in that indispensable professional, The Plumber. Sometimes it's because of a busted pipe, or a problem that obviously requires more equipment and expertise than we possess. Other times, it may be due to our overwhelming laziness.

Whatever prompts you to make that call, there are some things you should know beforehand. Those of you who have gone through the drill are already aware of this, but may wish to use the following as a refresher course.

There are two things you need to do before requesting a plumber—and you never *order* one, you *request* one. First check your bank account or credit card limit. This may well prevent an embarrassing moment once the work is done, or a possible court battle later. And do not think for a moment, plumbers can't take back the work they've done. They were taught how to do that in Cheapskates 101 at Plumb U.

The second thing to consider is the type of plumber you need. Is your problem small enough to call on a general plumber, or will you need a specialist? A general plumber can show you how to mix the hot and cold water together for a comfortable shower, read your water bill, and the proper way to drain a bathtub.

For most other problems you will need to call on a specialist. With advancements in water technology—not to mention the new theories about gravity and how they could affect our morning constitutions—the plumbing industry is hard pressed to keep up with it all. New fields in the profession are continually being introduced, and improvements in existing plumbing are changing almost daily.

Plumbers specialize in such fields as new or old plumbing, indoor or outdoor, incoming or outgoing, bathroom or kitchen, hot water or cold water, and stocked or un-stocked wet bar plumbing to name just a few. After the plumber has granted your request to come to your house and give you an estimate, prepare your home carefully. The plumber's first impression of your financial status will have a profound effect on your estimate. You want to give the impression you can afford the services without running out to hold up a liquor store, but you're not so affluent as to invite an open-ended work order.

Begin your preparations with the outside of your house. Pick up all empty beer cans and beer bottles in the front yard. If you have a vehicle on cinder blocks, move it to your neighbor's backyard.

If your house is in bad need of a paint job, brush on several small streaks of different colors next to the front door, and say you are trying to decide which color to paint the place. Do not ask the plumber's preference. You may be expected to begin the paint job.

Make sure you remove all trash, even if you didn't throw it there. If your lawn has more weeds than grass, make a sign that reads, *NATURE PRESERVE*.

Put your real name on the mailbox.

For the interior of your home, pick up all empty beer cans and beer bottles. Especially in the areas where the plumber will have to walk or work.

Take down all black velvet paintings, even the ones of Elvis. If you happen to fall into the top one percent income bracket and own original Rembrandts, or any other kind of art by one of the Old Masters, conceal them carefully. Your estimate may hinge on not only how destitute you look, but also on how filthy rich you appear.

If you can find one, hang a picture of Thomas Crapper on the wall.

Choose a clean, quiet room for hearing the plumber's estimate. It should have a large table and comfortable chairs. This will be where you receive the plumber's explanation of your catastrophic plumbing problem and how, for a rock bottom price, you can once again enjoy your life. This room is also where you will nonchalantly pay that rock bottom price. Assuming, of course, you are still in control of your nonchalance at that point. Choose well.

On the big day, take care with your appearance for the occasion. Remove all studs from your ears, lips, and any other places they might show. Hide all other jewelry, except for a plain, gold wedding ring. If the ring is new, scuff it up a bit to look like you've had it on forever.

Avoid flashy colors. Remember, neutrality is your goal here—not a fashion statement. Wear brown or beige. A noncommittal gray is also acceptable.

Greeting the plumber is one of those all-important first impression moments. If your doorbell does not work, hide where you can see the front porch. When the plumber comes to the door, yank it open right before the button is pushed. Act surprised, and say you were just on your way next door to help the elderly bedridden widow wash her dishes or something. Don't forget to draw attention to the paint streaks next to the door, and your indecision on the color you want to paint the house.

If the doorbell works, stand out of sight until the plumber hears the melodic chimes. Control your nervousness and answer the door in a timely manner with a large smile. Take care not to look like a grinning idiot. Again, remember the upcoming paint job.

Once the plumber has looked over your problem and worked out a set of figures, you will both retire to the Estimate Room for the serious part of the negotiations. Of course the word *negotiations* in this case is somewhat misleading. You might be able to negotiate your method of payment, on which day you want the work to begin, or whether to use the plumber's pen or your own to sign on the dotted line. The price itself is not negotiable.

In order to perhaps sway the plumber's price in your favor, prepare in advance an assortment of snacks for the table. Since you won't know the background or preferences of the plumber, assemble a tasteful variety of tidbits. Lay out a decorative plate of freshly baked oatmeal cookies on a lace doily. Beside that, a pile of Slim Jims. Situate both tastefully next to a crystal bowl of caviar and gourmet crackers. Graciously offer them all.

This is not a time for frivolity. You're dealing in high finances here. You must maintain your dignity, but with a generous amount of respect and awe. Think an audience with the Pope, Queen Elizabeth, or Judge Judy.

After you have been given an estimate for the job, do not say you want to think it over. To a trained plumber, this instantly translates into, "I'm going to get another quote." Competitors or not, the BoPs (Brotherhood of Plumbers) respect each other when it comes to undercutting a fellow BoPs' estimate. The original plumber quoting a price will leave an almost invisible coded message somewhere on your house that alerts other BoPs of the previous quote. As of this writing, neither the CIA nor the NSA has broken that code.

Eventually, you will either accept the original bid or, out of spite, settle for a higher one from a different plumber. Keep in mind *spite* is a powerful weapon. Before you pull that trigger take a good look at who it's really pointing at.

When the work begins it makes no difference if you went with your spite, or good sense. You still need to stay on your toes. Even with a contract for a set price, your plumbing could have other serious problems only an experienced plumber can uncover. You may not be aware of this, but your plumber certainly is.

Five rules of etiquette to follow once the actual work commences:

Don't offer to help.

Don't crack any cleavage jokes when your plumber is bent over while working–especially if your plumber is a she, or any other kind of plumber with a frontal cleavage.

Don't offer finger foods to snack on while your plumber is working.

Don't underestimate your plumber's intelligence. She or he probably owns a second home in the country and drives a customized Ferrari.

Don't ever say some of your best friends are plumbers.

When paying your bill with a check, never look at your balance. Casually make out the check as if you're accustomed to routinely writing such large figures. Practice doing this in the privacy of your car, attic, or some other place the plumber is unlikely to see you. If you plan to use a credit card, practice whipping it out of your wallet in a smooth and casual manner as if you use it all the time at Niemen Marcus.

Whichever payment method you use, control your shaking hand and try not to break out in a sweat. They can sense fear and know the opportune moment to try to sell you an extended warranty on the work, or to give you odds on how long before you'll have another plumbing problem.

If you should happen to lose control and show fear, respond to the extended warranty offer by saying you are putting the house up for sale. Politely decline the bet by stating you are a monk in training and are forbidden to gamble. If the plumber insists you choose one or the other, go for the bet and get the best odds you can.

After you have settled up with the plumber, there are a few things you need to do before you can return to a normal life. First, get your car and cinder blocks back, and take down that NATURE PRESERVE sign. You can leave the different colored paint streaks by the door for any future questions about the condition of your house paint.

Feel free to rehang your velvet paintings. Even the one of Elvis. As far as any Old Masters' art works, you probably would not have read this in the first place if you could afford any of those things.

Next, see about a loan before your check hits the bank, or if you are now unable to meet the minimum payment on your credit card after the plumbing repair charge.

And finally, replace your real name on the mailbox to Thomas Crapper.

End

EETOM

One of my mushrooms got loose the other day. Chaos reigned around the place for several hours before I managed to safely recapture it. That's the big problem with raising "shrooms," as we in the trade call them. No matter how well you treat them, or how nice you make their surroundings, they are not easily domesticated. They prefer living in the wild. Even after many generations of pampered living, deep down they still have a wild streak.

Most people are unaware of the true nature of mushrooms. They usually see live ones only when they're nestled in little plastic covered trays in the supermarket looking docile and content. Or they've seen them sliced, diced, or chopped in gravy over a steak, or in a myriad of other culinary delights. Of course, you can't see the canned mushrooms, but when you open the can, you still expect that serene look about them. Whether they're whole or in pieces.

This serenity look is no accident. We professional shroomers go to great lengths to breed it into our herds. Naturally, it means we must first eliminate the wild streak. That takes time and lots of patience.

Some unscrupulous shroomers, however, take shortcuts to achieve that look. Instead of patiently doing selective breeding, they turn to inhumane methods to subdue their mushrooms into temporary serenity. They place short term profits above all else. These are not honest professionals. They are merely cruel opportunists with their sights set only on the bottom line.

I will not go into detail about their methods. Suffice it to say they are shocking. At times, literally.

Some of the local shroomers and I tried to get an animal rights group to step in and end the horror. But PETA spokesfolks washed their hands of the whole affair. They claimed mushrooms were not classified as animals—even though many dedicated vegans have taken an oath not to eat mushroom gravy on their steaks.

That prompted we conscious-minded shroomers to band together and form an organization to promote consumer awareness on the mistreatment of innocent mushrooms. As with any organization worth its salt, the first order of the day is to come up with an acronym people will associate with your goals. We thought of calling ourselves People for the Ethical Treatment of Shrooms (PETS). But it looked too much like PETA, and we weren't on very good terms with them after they refused to help us. They can get pretty nasty with those who don't agree with them.

After kicking around a number of ideas, we finally settled on EETOM, which stands for Everybody for the Ethical Treatment Of Mushrooms.

Our first action was to confront the major supermarket chains. We loudly voiced our displeasure over their practice of buying mushrooms from people who brutalized and tortured them. We demanded more compassion from the supermarket managers who bought the lower priced mushrooms from those heartless dealers. We implored them to stock only humanely produced mushrooms in

Roy L Cover

their produce departments. And, of course, the ones stuffed into cans and placed on shelves in their canned goods section.

Unfortunately, our protests were unable to penetrate the ears of profit hungry CEOs. We then turned to a more drastic measure we all regret now. We brought out the placards and picketed all the major supermarkets in town. With our small membership, and the large number of stores, we could picket each one for only about ten minutes at a time in order to cover all of them in one day. Even so, we were too successful.

In our desperation to help the mushrooms, we caused a temporary market shortage of them. Like with a shortage of any consumer good, people immediately began to stock up. Even people who didn't like mushrooms, or had never even tasted one, frantically bought every mushroom in sight. Fresh, canned, or in gravy.

This shortage was immediately pounced upon by the very scoundrels we were trying to put out of business. They used every unimaginable and foul method in their dark minds to produce more and more mushrooms at an even faster pace.

We at EETOM were horrified and ashamed over the increased mistreatment we had set in motion. There was nothing left for us to do but admit defeat in our noble efforts. We called for a peace summit between ourselves and our hated enemies. It looked like the mushrooms last chance.

The one thing in our favor at the summit was EETOM was organized, unlike the ragtag barbarians who advocated brutality for the sake of profits. Little good it did us, though. The swine would agree to nothing. We were forced to walk away from the summit with nothing other than our honor and good name. That, and our tails tucked between our legs.

So, now it's up to you honorable consumers to stop the torture of defenseless mushrooms everywhere. You can do your part by buying only those mushrooms raised and loved by members in good standing of EETOM.

When in a restaurant that serves mushrooms, politely—but firmly—demand assurance all the mushrooms used were purchased only from EETOM approved suppliers.

And before buying fresh mushrooms at a farmer's market or your favorite supermarket, always look for "EETOM Approved" gently stamped on every mushroom's tender little bottom.

I thank you, and tasty mushrooms everywhere thank you.

End

A REALLY GREAT AUTO MECHANIC

I would never have built a birdhouse if it hadn't been for the really great mechanic I found a couple of months ago.

It was time for an oil change in my trusty little compact and I had nothing planned on that Saturday morning. Still, I didn't want to wait in line an hour-and-a-half for the guaranteed five-minute oil change at my local *Zippity Zoom Oil Change* franchise.

Then I remembered someone at the office a while back had talked about an auto repair shop not far from where I lived. I didn't catch too many details about the conversation except the part about a really great mechanic there. It seemed like a good time to check it out. Never can tell when you might need your car fixed, and that isn't the time to start looking for an honest mechanic.

When I drove up to *Uncle Ben's Auto Care*, a young man hurried out and stood next to my car. He wore freshly pressed mechanic's overalls and a wide grin. There was a small black grease smudge on his left cheek in the shape of an exclamation mark without the dot. He wiped his hands on a shop rag as he bent down a bit to look me in the eye.

"Hi there. I'm Uncle Ben. What can I do for you today?"

He seemed a little young to be an uncle of mine, and I thought it kind of odd his hands and the rag he was wiping them with were both clean. Still, I just couldn't resist that sincere smile. There was no doubt in my mind this was the honest mechanic I had been looking for.

"Hi, Uncle Ben. Would it be too much trouble to change the oil in my car this morning?"

Before I realized it, he had opened my car door and yanked me out with an enthusiastic, "Why, of course not. Just come with me to the customer waiting room."

He gently, but firmly, guided me to the small waiting room as he motioned to someone out of sight. "Barney will take care of your car. What did you say your name was?"

"Mark."

"What a coincidence! My grandfather's name was Mark. He was the warmest and most generous man I've ever known. I loved him so much."

"He's no longer with us?"

"No. Sadly, he died in an automobile accident when his brakes failed."

"I'm so sorry for your loss."

"Thank you. His accident made me become a mechanic. I swore I'd devote my whole life to make sure something like it never happens to anyone else."

"Um, that's quite a swore. Or swear. Or, uh. . . .But how do you go about it by just repairing cars?"

"It's not just repairing them, Mark. It's making sure they are safe to drive."

"But you can't make sure every car in the country is safe."

"No, but I can make sure all the cars that come into my shop are safe."

Somehow I missed the implications in his statement. "Well, it's an admirable goal, Uncle Ben. But all I need today is an oil change."

"Probably what Grampa Mark said on his last day on this earth. And good brakes would've saved his life."

It seemed necessary to respond, so I blurted out, "I had new brakes installed on my car just four months ago."

"Very wise of you, Mark. Now make yourself comfortable in here while Barney changes that oil for you." He flashed his sincere smile again and closed the door behind him.

Uncle Ben's waiting room was not much different from waiting rooms everywhere. There were no windows to the outside world and it was uncomfortably warm. A television perched on a shelf was tuned to a weather channel. No sound came from it, and there was no way to turn it up or change the channel.

Reading material on the wobbly coffee table consisted of a 1998 magazine for expectant mothers, two about new car reports from six years ago, one on building birdhouses, and several yellowed and worn magazines with the front covers torn off.

I settled for watching the silent TV and tried to understand the forecast of a foreign city. From the graphs and other artistic scribbles on top of what appeared to be Beijing, they seemed to be expecting either a monsoon, or a panda invasion. Whichever it was, the forecaster appeared quite excited about it.

Fortunately, or unfortunately, I didn't have long to wait before Uncle Ben came in wiping his still clean hands on the still clean rag. His grease smudge had moved to the right cheek. "Mark," he said in a grave voice, "did you know your alternator

34

belt is almost worn completely through?"

"As a matter of fact, I didn't." I hadn't planned on having any work done on the car that day, so I asked, "Do you think it will last for another few days?"

"You'd be taking a horrible chance. It could go at any moment. You might get stranded along a dark and stormy road in the middle of nowhere. At night."

"I don't usually go out of town."

"Oh, Mark. You sound just like my dear grampa on that fateful day."

"He had his accident in the middle of nowhere?"

"No. But he could have. His brakes would've failed no matter where he was. You see how serious this is?"

His sincerity was irresistible. "Maybe you'd better replace the belt then."

"You won't regret it, Mark." He gave me his reassuring smile and went to give Barney the good news. "We'll both sleep better tonight."

I hadn't considered coming in there for a better night's sleep. But since it came with an oil change, plus a new alternator belt, I wasn't going to complain.

The TV had switched from Beijing to what looked like Moscow. Or maybe Topeka. It was hard to tell if the city was in the middle of a blizzard, or there was interference on the TV. I picked up one of the new car reports magazine to see if mine was mentioned in it. The magazine was printed several years after my car was new.

That's when Uncle Ben rushed back in with his sincere smile wider than ever. "Mark, this is your lucky day."

"My car's ready?"

"Better yet." He sat down in the chair next to me, carefully folded his clean shop rag, and laid it in his lap. The grease smudge had returned to his left cheek. "Barney may very well have saved your life a few minutes ago."

I mentally reviewed the past few minutes, and could think of nothing more threatening to my life than a possible paper cut from the car magazine. But Barney wasn't even around to save me from that.

Uncle Ben filled me in on the terrifying details. "Barney had just finished installing your new alternator belt and was about to light up a cigarette—I know it's a bad habit and I've been trying to get him to stop. But he's such a great mechanic and he looks after my customers. Like you, Mark. I could never fire him for one little bad habit. You wouldn't want me to do something like that to someone who only wants you to be safe, would you?"

"Well, uh, no. Of course not."

"I didn't think so. I'd be disappointed if you did. Anyway, he was about to flick his Bic when he happened to glance over at the electromommeter on the bench. And do you know what he saw, Mark?"

After hearing all that drama, all I could do was close my mouth and shake my head.

"That electromometer was reading the highest level he had ever seen in his whole life."

"What did it mean?"

"Mean? It means your battery is leaking voltage all over the place! Who knows what would've happened to poor Barney if he had flicked his Bic."

"Poor Barney," was all I could think to add.

"But it could've been, 'Poor Mark,' if he hadn't been so alert."

"Me?"

"Yes. What if you had left here with that old battery leaking voltage all over the place, but there was no electromometer around to warn you of the danger?" He paused a moment. "And then you flicked *your* Bic. Humm?"

"I don't smoke."

"What if someone riding in your car flicked a Bic?"

"I don't allow smoking in my car."

"Mark, you're going into denial just like Grampa Mark did."

"He was in denial about his battery?"

"No, his brakes. I told you about that, remember?"

"Of course I remember. I'm so sorry for your loss."

"Thank you. But right now I'm concerned about you."

"You think my battery is as bad as your grandfather's brakes?"

"I'm afraid so. You see, voltage leaking all over the place leads to all kinds of problems."

"Like what?"

"For one thing, it has already caused the water in your radiator to go bad."

"It can go bad?"

"Of course it can. Haven't you ever heard of contaminated water before?"

"On TV a time or two. But I've never heard of it in connection with a radiator before."

He slowly shook his head. "That's the media for you. They only report half the story."

I had mixed feelings about this new problem, but at least water is fairly inexpensive. "How much is the battery?"

"How can you put a price on peace of mind, Mark?"

"Uh, actually it's my bank account that kinda puts a price limit on things."

"Then you might consider changing banks. We're talking about your mind here. And your life. Aren't those things important to you?"

"Of course they are. But—"

"Then it's settled. I have a great battery which happens to be on sale this week."

"But—"

"And don't worry about the contaminated fluid. I'll replace all of it with mountain fresh spring water. Free."

"Well gee, that's really nice of you, Uncle Ben."

He unfolded his shop rag, jumped up and headed for the door. On the way out of the waiting room he turned and added, "There'll be a small charge on your bill for the radiator water extractor, but it'll be so small you probably won't even notice it."

Before I could think of anything to say, or even close my mouth again, he was gone. The silent TV showed wind velocities and temperatures at various Antarctica weather stations. At least it made me thankful for the stifling heat in the waiting room. I picked up the birdhouse magazine and marveled at how the little houses looked like real ones, only in miniature. How strange it must be to live in another world.

Since there was no clock in the room, I had no idea how long it was before Uncle Ben returned with another way to save my life. The TV had run its full course back to Beijing, but judging by the weatherman's antics, neither the monsoon nor the pandas had arrived yet.

This time he opened the door and stood like an undertaker welcoming visitors to a wake. "I can't believe how lucky you are, Mark."

"There's another bad battery in my car?"

He thought for a moment before replying, "No, it's your tires."

"They're contaminated, too?"

"Of course not. When was the last time you had them rotated?"

"Well, uh. . ."

"Just what I thought. If you can't remember how long it's been, it's been too long."

"Do they really need it now?"

"Definitely." His grease smudge was back on his right cheek.

"They can't even go for a few more days?"

"They get more treacherous with every turn, Mark."

"But I only drive on good streets and freeways."

"Do you have any idea how many high speed accidents are caused by blowouts on the freeway?"

"I only drive the speed limit."

"Potholes can cause a blowout at practically any speed."

"The other roads I drive on are all in great condition."

"You're going into denial again, Mark."

"Sorry."

"Now I have a really cheap tire rotation deal today. It includes a thorough inspection of your brakes, struts, springs, stabilizers, and of course, the condition of the ion in your tires."

"There's supposed to be ion in my tires?"

It was Uncle Ben's turn to drop his mouth open. "Please don't tell me you've never had your tires ionized, Mark."

He had put me in a rather awkward situation. Not only had I never ionized my tires, I had never heard of such a thing. To make matters worse, he didn't want me to tell him that. I decided to fess up and tell him anyway. "Nobody ever told me I should."

Uncle Ben slowly shook his head and wiped his clean hands on the still clean rag. "Mark," he said in a gentle voice as he walked over and sat in the chair next to me. He put his arm around my shoulders and drew me close. "You have been done a great disservice by many people when it comes to taking care of your automobile."

"I have?"

"Absolutely. And you must have a guardian angel sitting on your shoulder to keep you from winding up like my dear Grampa Mark."

"What do you mean?"

"Why, the way you've cheated the Grim Reaper for so long in that death trap of yours."

"Death trap? My car?"

"Oh, Mark. Haven't you noticed every time Barney tries to fix something on your car he discovers yet another impending disaster? How many times must he save your life before you step out of that four-door denial you've been riding around in?"

"It's a two door."

"That's not important. I simply can't bear to see another Mark in my life ending up in a tangled mass of metal all on account of his blind denial."

I didn't want to bring up the painful memory of his grandfather again, but I had to ask, "Was your Grandpa Mark in denial at. . .at the end?"

He dabbed at his eyes with his still clean rag. "I didn't see him on his last day. He was celebrating his ninety-fourth birthday at a strip club on the east side of town. After Happy Hour was over he headed back home, but I'm sure he was in as much denial about being blind drunk as he was about his bad brakes."

His emotional response was almost too much to bear. I was

ashamed of myself for bringing up such an obviously agonizing part of his life. In my most sincere way, I said, "I'm so sorry for your loss."

"Thank you." He sniffed and patted me on the shoulder. "I'll tell Barney to ionize your tires, but I won't charge you for it. Your safety is worth more to me than mere dollars."

As if that wasn't enough to choke me up, his next statements certainly did.

"You know, Mark, it isn't only your name that reminds so much of my dear, dear grandfather."

I could think of no response other than to slowly shake my head.

"It's your car."

"My car?"

He dabbed at his eyes again with the rag. "Yes. Grampa Mark's car was exactly like yours. Except for the number of doors. But I won't trouble you anymore with my heart-wrenching memories." He sighed, slowly stood up, and slowly walked toward the door with his head down.

I could take no more of his grief.

"Uncle Ben, wait. I need to go home and feed my goldfish and my cat now, but can I leave my death. . .I mean my car here so you can do whatever it takes to make it safe?"

His veil of sadness was instantly replaced with his sincere smile as he turned around. "Mark, you'll remember this decision for the rest of your life."

Now, as the weeks pass, his words ring more true with every ring of my phone. At first his calls advised me of little things my car needed. It seems every filter on my death trap needed to be replaced. Then the headlights needed adjustment, which lead to the discovery they were woefully inadequate when he conjured up images of the dark and stormy deserted road in the middle of nowhere again. At night. Fortunately, he had some brighter headlights on sale at the time.

The problems grew more and more serious. The only saving grace about it all was Barney had a certificate of one kind or another to overcome whatever impending disaster he uncovered. And most all of the problems were solved with a special sale of one sort or another. Always fortunately, of course.

All this attention devoted to keeping me safe from my murderous death trap has allowed me to concentrate on other things in my life. Things like whether or not the tufted titmouse will like the split level birdhouse I plan to build. I should have enough time to finish it before Uncle Ben calls to let me know Barney has finished re-calibrating my transmission, and will take the car out for another test drive.

Then, Uncle Ben will make the inevitable call to let me know how Barney can, once more, save my life.

End

OVER THE HILL

They tell me I'm over the hill now. Hell fire, I didn't even know I'd reached the top of the damn thing. And now I'm over it. All downhill from here. You'd think it would mean easier going from now on. Not a chance. There's no end of the rocks on the way down. And you don't even know how far down "down" is. Of course I didn't know how far up the hill went, either.

But here I am on the way down. Makes me wish I'd built a little better sled for the trip. One with wheels. Springs would've been nice, too. The kind they put in a Rolls Royce. I'd settle for a little cardboard padding right about now.

The downhill trip means more regular visits to the clinic now, too. Folks are nice there, though. Too damn nice. Treat me like a lost two-year old at a funeral. I keep expecting them to kiss me on top of the head every time one of them talks to me.

It all starts when I enter the clinic and the receptionist greets me with her sugary, "Good morning!"

Was till I had to come here. "And good morning to you."

"I see you're right on time, as usual."

Amazing I can still tell time even though I'm over the hill, isn't it? "Don't like to be late for things, you know."

"Did you remember to bring all your medications with you?"

43

As much as they cost, you think I'd let 'em out of my sight? "Sure did."

"Good. Just have a seat in the waiting room. We'll call you when the doctor is ready to see you."

Hell fire, he's had as much time to get ready as I have. "Okay."

Then it's the waiting room. The one with no clock. As if nobody has any way of figuring out how long they have to sit there before they're called into a smaller room to wait another unknown time. I fool the hell out of them. I've got an infallible internal clock. Plus, I wear a wristwatch.

I always bring a book along to read while the doctor is getting ready to see me, even though a lot of waiting rooms now have televisions. Not the kind showing uplifting and entertaining things like the all-weather channel, though. These TVs play only special health-related things.

You know the kind. These come on like an infomercial. They usually star a guy and a gal telling you how to live longer and healthier, and how to deal with old age. Their combined age looks to be about forty-five.

They start off by saying you should run, walk, or ride a bike about ten miles every day. Then with a straight face, one of them, usually the gal, will say you can relax at the end of the day by standing on your head, or lying on the floor and tying yourself in a knot.

Before the two beautiful people finish flashing their perfect pearly whites, they have a few words about nutrition. It seems this country has it all wrong when it comes to feeding our face. I've lost track of how many little countries and islands around the world grow magic beans, berries, or buttercups that keep you from going over the hill for a hundred years. Maybe more.

After these astonishing claims there is usually a short clip showing some brown-skinned people flashing toothless grins in front of a mud hut. They look really, really old, but they might only be in their thirties. Hard to tell with the hard life folks must have who live in a mud hut.

In a regular infomercial, the announcer would probably tell you a thirty-day supply of these miracle goodies will cost you only nineteen-ninety-five. Plus shipping and handling. But you also get a free booklet telling you how to cook the stuff. Maybe even throw in some tips on how to exercise.

The waiting room TV doesn't sell things, though. The bubbly duo gives me free information on picking up these miracle munchies at specialty food stores, or I can ask my local grocer to stock them for me. The only local grocers I regularly talk to are the ones who stock the chips and donuts, or take my money. None of them strike me as the type who would have the faintest idea what any of that junk is, or how to get it if they did know.

After the dynamic duo give their cheerful goodbyes, some guy in a tailored suit comes on the screen and claims to be doctor so-and-so. He very well could be a real doctor. There's not a patient anywhere around him.

While the well-dressed guy drones on about whatever he thinks is important, I usually check out the other folks who are also waiting for their doctor to get ready to see them. They generally fall into one of two main groups.

The first group is made up of the yappy ones. They insist on finding out who you are, where you come from, and why you're there. Then they make sure you know no matter what ails you, they have it too. But ten times worse and for twice as long. And they go on to tell you all the other things wrong with them and the rest of their family. They will, if you don't get up and go to the can.

The second bunch consists of the silent type. You never know what kind of malady they might be carrying around. They usually tend to cough a lot. I also go to the can whenever one of them sits close to me. Then find another place to sit.

One time when I got back from the can and sat in an empty chair, I found myself between a yakker and a hacker. I was about ready to go to the can again. Only this time it was going to be my can at home.

But just then my name came over the scratchy speaker. I clearly heard it above all the chattering and coughing. In that situation, I would've heard my name called if I sat in the front row of a rock concert and it was whispered from next door.

My elated feeling soon fades, though, with another sugary-talking nurse on the other side of the waiting room door.

"And how are we feeling today?"

Got a mouse in your pocket? I'm over the hill. How the hell do you think I feel? "Fine."

"Can you make it over here to the scales by yourself, so we can see how much you weigh today?"

I made it over the damn hill by myself, I guess I can climb your puny scale by myself. "Yes, I can manage okay. Thank you."

"My, looks like we put on a couple of pounds since you were here last."

Yeah, just wait till you and your mouse get over the hill. "I guess I fudged a bit on my diet."

"Now we can't have that, you know."

Tell it to your mouse. "I'll do better. I promise."

"I know you will. Now just have a seat over there and let me take your blood pressure, while I ask you a few questions."

Let's see if I can make it that far after climbing those scales. "Okay."

"Have you fallen lately?"

Oh god, yes. I fell asleep again last night. "No."

"Do you have trouble sleeping?"

Just the falling part. "No."

"Have you suffered from any loss of appetite?"

Did you already forget what those scales said? "No."

"Have you had any feelings of depression?"

Only about coming here. "No."

"I'm going to give you four words to remember, and I'll ask you to repeat them to me before you leave today, okay?"

As if I have a choice. "Okay."

"Coat, book, red, and thought. Would you like me to repeat them for you?"

Why don't you just get a parrot? "Would they be, 'coat, book, red, and thought?'"

"Yes. Very good. And your blood pressure is fine this morning. You must be taking your medications regularly."

Either that, or you, me, and your mouse have just seen a miracle. "Like clockwork."

"Good for you. Now, if you'll just follow me to the exam room."

God, I hope your memory has improved since the scales incident. I'd hate to keep following you around while you try to remember where the hell the exam room is. "Just lead the way."

"Okay, just have a seat on the table here. The doctor will be with you shortly."

I wish your shortly meant the same as my shortly. "Thank you."

Then the secondary wait begins. Only now there aren't those other distractions so entertaining in the big waiting room. That's when the book comes in handy.

Eventually, my doctor manages to get good and ready to see me and glances at my chart.

"Minor emergency came up. Hope you haven't been waiting too long."

That depends. What day is it now? "Not at all."

"How are we feeling today?"

Must be a rodent problem in here, too. "Fine."

"I see you've put on a couple of pounds since you were here last."

Would've been more if I could've been home eating instead of coming here. "Yeah, guess I succumbed to temptation a little."

"Don't you realize the importance of watching your weight at your age?"

Hey, I watch it every time I try to button my pants. "I know it's important, but I just can't keep to the diet you gave me."

"I know it's hard. Tell you what, if I include more of some of the things you like, would you be willing to try a little harder?"

Oh, jeez, if I come up with a counter offer, will he have to consult his manager? "What do you have in mind?"

"A little indulgence now and then of your favorite foods won't hurt. The key is to indulge infrequently and sparingly."

Indulge, I understand. Your infrequently and sparingly befuddles the hell out of me. "What all can it include?"

"Let's see. What are some of your favorite foods?"

Hmm, that would include anything with a lot of grease and calories. "Well, I like ice cream, donuts, and beer."

48

"All right, you could occasionally have some ice cream. There are a number of low calorie ice creams on the market these days."

Occasionally? And low calorie and ice cream in the same sentence? "How many quarts could I have in a week?"

"Seriously, now."

You mean you haven't been serious till now? "So what you're saying is, it should be pints per week instead of quarts?"

"Most assuredly not quarts."

I assume that applies to whiskey as well. "Just a little joke, Doc,"

"Well, all joking aside, you could have a small bowl of low cal ice cream now and then."

The now part I get, but how soon before the then part gets back to the now part? "I understand." *Except for low cal and ice cream in the same sentence.*

"What else are you having trouble cutting back on?"

Trips to this clinic. "How many donuts can I have for breakfast?"

"Have you tried a piece of toast with a dab of honey on it instead?"

Hmm, haven't tried that. Or chewing on an old sock, either. "No, but it's an idea."

"See? There's a lot of healthy substitutes out there."

Wonder what I could substitute for the liqueur I pour over my stack of waffles? "I see."

"Anything else you overindulge in?"

Unfortunately, not nearly as many things as I used to. "How about beer?"

"Not more than one a day."

Finally, some good news. "One six pack? What kind of look is that?"

"I think you know what it means. One beer per day. . .a twelve-ounce beer."

The doctor giveth, and the doctor yanketh away. "I understand."

"Good, because all these things are very important. Is your last prescription working out okay?"

The drug store seems to be happy about the price. "Just great. Never felt better."

"Okay. We'll just continue with it for now."

So you're taking them too? Or are you including the mouse? "Fine."

"Do you have any other questions?"

Now that you ask, why was I born so good looking instead of rich? "Can't think of any."

"All right, we'll see you again next month. And try a little harder to stick to your diet."

I look forward to seeing you and your mouse again then. "I'll try."

The good doctor is then off to let some other lucky person know he's ready to see him or her.

Enter the nurse with her clipboard, her mouse, and her bad memory.

"So we'll see you again next month."

If your mouse doesn't kick the bucket before then. "You bet."

"But before you go, do you remember those four words I asked you to repeat for me?"

Yeah, but you probably won't be satisfied unless I say them out loud. "Coat, book, red, and, and let me think. . ."

"Oh, you're so funny."

50

Comes with gettin' over the hill. "Just for the record, you know I was thinking about 'thought,' right?"

"Of course. Now you have a nice day!"

That's my cue this clinic visit is over. All I have left now is the friendly receptionist and her parting sugar on my way out.

"Have a nice day. We'll see you again next month."

Take good care of our mice. "Don't take any wooden nickels."

"Oh, you're so funny."

Says the recording with a laugh track.

Then it's out the door to continue my slide down that damn hill. Should've brought my umbrella. Starting to rain.

It sure is a pretty day.

End

WHEN NYE BECAME NAY

Problem number one for the original civic committee meeting came when taking the first floor vote, as its following minutes illustrate.

"All those in favor say, *Aye*.

"Those opposed say, *Nye*.

"I'm sorry, but it's too close to tell with a voice vote. All those who wish to vote *Aye* raise your hand.

"All right. Now those who wish to vote with a *Nye* raise your hand.

"No, no. Those of you who already voted with an *Aye* put your hand down. Just those who wish to vote with a *Nye* now raise your hand.

"No, you're doing it all wrong again. Listen to me. If you want to vote *Aye* raise your hand. Good. Now put your hands down. Very good. Now, all of you who wish to vote with a *Nye* raise your hand.

"No, *no!* What is *wrong* with you people?"

Hence the floor vote became *Aye* and *Nay*. But it's questionable as to whether it did much to improve committee efficiency.

End

THE R.I.P. X-PRESS

The abrupt end to my peaceful vacation and the start of a bizarre summer began early one morning when my cousin paid me a visit.

"It can't miss," Charlie had said as he breezed through my back door into the kitchen, and promptly rummaged through my fridge. He settled on a carton of orange juice and a leftover chicken leg.

Charlie would not be my first choice for a cousin if such things were possible, but sometimes life likes to play little jokes on us.

He carried his breakfast feast over and flopped down at the table across from me. "Folks are gonna break down our door for this."

At his mention of the word *our*, I should've immediately got up and gone bowling or something. Anytime he used the words *we* or *our* meant a drain on my bank account and another step closer to an ulcer. But Charlie is such a likable guy, and I was still on my first cup of coffee.

"Couldn't they just knock?" I asked.

"Who?"

"All those people who'll want to break down my door down for, uh . . .?"

He finally caught the idea behind my inquisitive stare and silence and said, "Oh. You mean the folks who'll want our *Last Ride Funeral Service?*"

"Our, I mean, the what?"

"*Last Ride Funeral Service*." He took a bite of the chicken and a drink of juice from the carton, and added, "Oh yeah, my Mom said to tell you, 'Hello.'"

Whether his mother, my aunt, had actually sent the greeting or not, I knew my fate was sealed and I would be a part in his latest hair brained idea. She conveniently reminded me at times like this Charlie had saved my life and I owed him big time. Her recounting of the events has always been a little vague, and the details seem to change a little at each telling, but it all revolved around a birthday party, spiked punch, and a pin-the-tail-on-the-donkey game. I don't remember any of it. Charlie and I must've only been around three or four at the time.

I got up, poured myself another cup of coffee, and returned to the table. "I take it this door breaking has something to do with a funeral?"

"Got everything to do with one," he answered. "That's why 'Funeral' is in the company name."

I took a big drink of coffee. "Don't know how I missed that."

He went into one of his deep thought moments while I took another cobweb chasing shot of coffee. Then, "Maybe we need a catchier name."

"Like *Acme's* whatever," which I thought was sarcastic enough.

After another short deep thought moment, he brightened and said, "That's it. But we need a name with more respectfully. Like yours, Leo."

I wasn't about to argue over the respectability of my name. I needed more coffee and poured myself another cup. But I had a growing suspicion there wasn't enough coffee in the world to get me out of this.

"Here's all we gotta do—"

"What *you* have to do, Charlie, not *we*."

"Right. We know they already got those drive-through funeral places. You know, where you can drive up to a big picture window and look at the person that's dead, and pay your respects or whatever, and drive off. Never have to even get out of the car. Don't have to dress up or nothing. Don't wear shoes if you don't wanna."

I started to explain how expensive something like that would be, but he got all excited and his voice reached a high irritating pitch like an electric motor that's about to seize up.

"This here's the best part," he raced on. "We go after the folks that don't got no car. Or the ones don't like to drive. Maybe they don't got the time to drive all over town just to look at somebody that's dead."

I started to interrupt, but he sprang out of his chair. "All we need is a van."

He drew an imaginary outline in the air with the chicken leg of what he visualized to be a van.

"One with windows."

He added a couple of air windows that looked a little too big for the van.

"We just load up the stiff."

He slid a body into the back of the van and closed the door.

"Then we haul it around to the places the guy used to go to before he got dead."

Charlie sat back down with a big smile, took the last bite of the chicken leg, and finished the juice. He aimed for the trash, but the bone missed. It took me a couple of moments to recover from his presentation before I said, "I was under the impression they still had a vehicle for something like that. It's called a hearse."

His smile didn't fade. "Sure, but those things just do the hauling. We got the thing that does the *showin'*. I got this undertaker friend told me everything we need to know about hauling dead people around. I figured out how we can do the showin' part."

He saw by my slack mouth he had lost me. He stood up, placed his hands on the imaginary van, and gently pushed it out of the way as he went into his second act. "Just think about it, Leo. All the buddies of this guy," he pointed toward the parked van, "can look at him without taking time off from work, or driving all over town. Heck, even guys what didn't like him all that much can look 'cause they can do it without missing doing something else they'd rather be doing."

Had it been anyone other than Charlie going on like that, I would have been very uncomfortable being alone in the same room with him. Maybe I was stunned by the whole morbid affair, or maybe he had already thrown in too many *we's* by this time. Whatever the reason, I failed to end the insanity before it got completely out of control.

"Who do you think is going to pay for this kind of. . .of service?" I asked.

Charlie walked over behind me, put his hands on my shoulders, and placed his mouth next to my ear. "Leo," he whispered, "it is everyone's duty to pay their last respects to the recent departed. And that," indicating the air van with a nod of his head, "is how we're gonna make that possible for every man, woman, and kid in the whole wide town."

He had stunned me again. Only this time I recovered quicker, and asked what I thought was the death-knell question to this lunacy. "How are you going to make any money doing this?

"This is the best part," he said as he sat down wringing his hands like the villain in a cheap horror movie. "We go after the dead guys that used to work for some big factory. Then we go straight up to the boss and tell him we can bring the stiff right to the job. That way everybody can have a look and not take off work. He'll save a bundle."

"You plan to drive this thing through a *factory*?"

"Don't be crazy, Leo. We do it at break time. Pull the van right in behind the lunch wagon. Guys can get their sandwiches and chips and Twinkees and coffee, then walk right by the van and look at the dead guy."

"You honestly believe a company would pay for such a thing?"

"Sure they'll pay. Pay a lot, too. Especially after a good sales pitch. You know, like the kind you're so good at, Leo."

Charlie always knows when to throw logic my way. Along with his cheap flattery.

He must have known at that point he had drawn me completely into his foggy world. He walked to the cupboard and took out a bag of chips and ripped them open. After filling his hand, and then his mouth, he talked around the chips as he chewed.

"There's more. Know all those bars around town? They're always lookin' for ways to bring folks in. Work a deal with them. We bring the van around with a dead guy that used to be a customer. Don't even have to been a customer. Just tell 'em the guy used to drink. Drunks all look alike after a few drinks anyway. Right?"

Even though he meant it as a rhetorical question, I nodded, which gave him a chance to catch his breath and refill his mouth with chips before going on. "We tell the bartender we're bringing around an old drinking buddy for one last round. It'll pack 'em in like a Tokyo subway at rush hour. We should be able to hit a dozen bars in one night with the same stiff. Give 'em all a good price, too. Maybe even put a contribution box next to the van so all the folks who did him wrong can kinda make amens for it."

Looking out through Charlie's fog I nodded again, completely ignoring the fact the deceased could not possibly resemble someone familiar to *everyone*. Logic had moved beyond my grasp as I mentally began working on a sales pitch. The kind I'm so good at.

The next day I signed a note on a used van, sight unseen. Charlie had looked it over from bumper to bumper, and assured me it was exactly what we needed—plus a fifteen-hundred-dollar check from me for a few minor adjustments. It put a strain on my budget, and my bank account, but he swore I would see the money back within two weeks. As he pointed out, I would be off vacation by then and have a steady income again to pick up the slack.

"What do you mean, 'slack?'"

"Just a business word, Leo. All big shots use it when they start up. Don't mean nothin' really important."

With that, he grabbed the note and check, and headed out to pick up the van. I asked to go along, but he wanted to take it to one of his friends first who would make it into something *professional*, as he put it.

To kill some time and get into the swing of the new business, I searched through the daily obituaries for possible clients.

Two days later Charlie burst through my back door and grabbed me by the arm. "Come look at this, Leo."

He pulled me out to the backyard and swung his arm in a grand gesture that encompassed our van. "What do you think?"

I stood in front of the faded red vehicle and made a couple of comments without mentioning all the dents and scratches. "The tires don't have any tread on them. And there aren't any wiper blades."

"No problem. We'll be parked most of the time. And we won't be doing any showin' when it's raining."

It was pointless to argue with that, but I did take issue with the lettering on the driver's side. "What in the soup bowl is *that*?"

He looked hurt. "It's our company name."

"Oh, no. Take it back to whoever did that and have them repaint it."

"But it shows the company's integrity."

"*Honest Leo's* shows integrity? Sounds like a used car lot. And the misspelling after that has got to go."

"It's just one word. Nobody will notice."

"You think nobody will notice *Honest Leo's Funreal Service*?"

"Okay. Okay. I'll take care of it. But first take a look at the showin' side."

Charlie led me around to the passenger side where I saw more creativity than I ever imagined from him. "Is that my aluminum storm door from the house?"

"Yeah, but I'll get you another one. You see, my friend is a carpenter and he didn't know how to put any other kind of window in the side of the van. And being in there sideways like this will let more folks look at the stiff."

That's when I looked through the window and saw a cardboard refrigerator box on its side. The top, bottom, and side had been cut down and painted brown, which made it look like a cheap imitation of a casket with no lid. Except it was only about a foot high. A corpse in a pair of checkered swim trunks was laid-out inside.

"What. . .who is that?"

"John."

"John who? And where did he come from?"

"John Doe. A friend of mine down at the city morgue let us borrow him before he got logged in."

My mouth opened and closed several times with nothing coming out.

Charlie cocked his head and put his face close to mine. "You feeling okay, Leo?"

The words finally came out. "That's it. No more. Quit. Done. It's all over."

"But we haven't even got rolling yet. We can take this guy around to some bars or—"

"No, we're not. We are going to take him back. And then you are going to tell your friend we don't want any more dead people."

I jumped into the passenger's bucket seat and noticed it wasn't firmly bolted to the floor. Charlie got in behind the wheel and started the engine. "You really sure you want to kill the company, Leo?"

"Please, don't use the word 'kill.' I've had all this morbid stuff I can stand. As far as I'm concerned, this company is dead. Now let's go."

It was a quiet ride on the way to the morgue. Except for the rattling and wheezing of the van. After several blocks Charlie said in a soft voice, "My mom called just before we left and said to tell you, 'Hi.'"

I wasn't sure if he knew that was below the belt or not, but I held firm. I rolled down the window and turned my attention to the passing sights to discourage any conversation, and to distract my conscience.

He stopped in the left-turn lane at an intersection when the light turned red. While we were waiting for the light to change, a blue car with a yellow front fender and hood stopped in the lane next to us. The two couples in it didn't pay us any attention until the driver jerked his thumb in our direction and said something to the others. The guy in the back seat looked like he was oddly related to the one driving. They both had that look of spending too much time squinting at the sun, and not enough time with a dentist. Their girlfriends, on the other hand, looked as if they had been very friendly with their dentist. And with many others besides.

Charlie turned left when the light changed. The car beside us went straight ahead, but not before I heard the shouts from it.

"That was Butch back there."

"You're crazy."

"Damn sure ought to know my own brother!"

I thought it best to hurry along to the morgue. "How much farther, Charlie?"

"About six blocks. But this is a waste of time."

I kept checking the outside mirror. "What are you talking about?"

"My friend works nights. He won't be there for another five hours. None of the other guys down there know anything about John."

"Why didn't you tell me before we left?"

"Thought maybe you'd change your mind before we got there."

"Oh, great. Are you sure this guy is really a 'John Doe?'"

"Sure I'm sure. My friend said he was found floating in the lake. Had nothing on him but swim trunks."

I let out a groan and slumped in my seat.

"You sick, Leo?"

"No. Just take us back to my house."

Charlie continued to stare at me. "You sure you're okay? You don't look so hot."

"Really, I'm—"

He turned his attention back to the street just in time to see a car pull out of an alley in front of us. He couldn't go around because of oncoming traffic, so he slammed on the brakes. The van made a sudden stop. John did not.

He was tossed forward between the seats and ended up in my lap with his arms and legs tangled all over me. His head rested on the dash.

I tried to sit back up in my seat to get enough leverage to push him back when I glanced through the outside mirror. The blue and yellow car rounded a corner a couple blocks behind us and headed our way.

"Step on it, Charlie!"

The van had pretty good get-up-and-go in spite of its looks. We were up to thirty-five in no time. Fortunately, the blue and yellow was no dragster, either.

"What's the big hurry, Leo?"

"We can't let that car catch us."

"The one behind us?"

"Yes. Ditch him."

Charlie stomped his foot on the accelerator, but not much happened. I managed to lift my head enough to see over the small section of the dash that John didn't occupy.

"Turn right at the next corner."

"But it's a one-way."

"I know. Turn anyway. Now!"

Our tires screeched as he spun the wheel to the right. More tires screeched as on-coming cars scattered out of our way. And John changed location.

Charlie now held John in his lap while he tried to see where we were going, which may have worked in our favor.

I did my best to give directions until I could pull John away and push him between the seats and into the back. By then we had reached an intersection and turned off the one-way street. I saw in the mirror the blue and yellow car had not been so lucky. It had become part of a several-car pileup.

"We sure gave 'em the slip didn't we, Leo?"

"Yeah, Charlie. We gave them the slip all right. The question now, is how long before they find the hideout of *Honest Leo's Funreal Service*?"

I had nothing to say on the way back to my house, and Charlie wisely kept his mouth shut. John, of course, had no choice but to keep quiet.

After the van was parked out of sight in my back yard, Charlie put John back in his makeshift casket and covered him up with one of my good blankets. Then he joined me in the kitchen. I sat at the table and watched him stick his head in the fridge. He rustled around until he brought out a bowl of leftover mashed potatoes and a milk carton.

He picked up a spoon and a glass from the sink and sat down across from me. "Is this milk okay, Leo?" he asked while he emptied the carton into the glass.

"Yeah. Just bought it a couple of days ago."

"Well, it smells funny."

Then I caught a whiff of something odd myself. I looked around and sniffed until I discovered the odor was coming from my clothes. "Oh, my God. It's John."

Charlie was still sniffing the milk. "John who?" Then he looked over at me. "Oh, yeah. John."

I hadn't noticed the smell in the van because the windows had been down. In the still air of the kitchen the odor from my clothes made it clear John was quietly trying to tell us something. He wanted to be underground. Soon.

"Get a hold of your friend at the morgue, Charlie. Maybe he can send a hearse or ambulance over here and take him back."

"But I don't know his home phone. I only see him nights at the morgue."

I didn't bother to ask why he spent his nights in such a place. "Call down there. Somebody must have his number."

Charlie brought out his wallet and spilled the contents on the table. It made an impressive pile of business cards, bits of scribbled-on napkins, and countless smudged paper scraps. Each piece had a phone number, but none of them had a name for the number.

"How can you tell who all those numbers go to?"

"Little trick a plumber friend of mine taught me. You look at the number real close when you write it down and think about the guy while you do it. Then whenever you see the number, you remember all the things you were thinking about when you wrote it down. Pretty cool, huh?"

I shook my head and watched him sift through the mess until he said, "Aha," and handed me one of the scraps of paper with a phone number on it. "Hold onto this."

"The morgue?"

"No," he answered as he continued to look through the pile.

"Friend of mine. Got a bail bond business."

I clenched my teeth, and took a deep breath through my nose, but kept quiet.

"Here it is," he said holding up a piece of paper like a trophy trout.

"Just dial it, Charlie."

I went into my bathroom, took a shower, and changed clothes. When I came back into the kitchen, John's odor still lingered. It came from Charlie's clothes. I went into my bedroom and rustled up a pair of pants and a shirt that were getting a little snug for me.

"You get his home number?" I asked, as I walked back into the kitchen and tossed the clean clothes on the table.

"Uh, we won't need it."

"He came in early?"

"Actually, he won't be coming in at all."

"You mean he quit?"

Charlie shook his head. "Jail."

"Because of John?"

"They didn't say."

A million things raced through my mind, but I couldn't pin anything down.

"You know, Leo, we got a little problem here."

Sarcasm was all I could come up with. "And just what *little* problem do we have, Charlie?"

"We got no more food in the fridge."

"No, Charlie. *I* have no more food in the fridge. And I have no more food, because you ate it all."

"Don't worry, Leo. I got a friend that runs a little grocery store. He'll give you all you want on credit. No questions asked. Even delivers. Got his number here somewhere."

"No, Charlie. I'm already in hock over my ears."

"Hey, we gotta eat. I'll just have him send over something. You know, just a few basics to tide us over till we make a couple of showings with John."

"Have you gone completely wacko on me? We can't take him anywhere with those people back there looking for us. Probably the cops, too, by now."

Charlie emptied his glass of milk, spooned out the last of the mashed potatoes from the bowl, and took another fruitless look in the fridge. "You mean those folks in that blue and yellow car?"

"You know good and well that's who—"

He laughed and opened the cupboard for a fruitless look in there. "Be a while before they go anywhere. Last I saw they was hanging off the front bumper of a UPS truck."

"Great. Now they have another reason to look for us. No doubt UPS will join the crowd."

"Don't worry, Leo," he said as he sat back down and sifted through his pile of numbers again. "They're all the way on the other side of town. By the time they get another car, we'll already have made some money from John, put him to rest, got rid of the van, and nobody will be none the smarter."

"Make *money* from him? How can you possibly think of taking him out in public again after all that?"

"C'mon, Leo, relax." He selected a scrap of paper from his pile of numbers. "Let me call my friend and have him send over some food. You'll feel better after you've had something to eat."

"My problem is not from hunger. My problem right now is how to get John back to the morgue. Then, I'll face the other things."

"But, we can't get rid of him just like that."

"Why not?"

"What about his dignity?"

"His what?"

"His *dignity*, Leo. We can't just dump him like yesterday's garbage. He needs a proper send-off."

"What are you babbling about now?"

"Respect, Leo. Would you want to be laid to rest by total strangers? No goodbye words? Nobody crying because you're gone? How would *you* feel if you were just 'got rid of' when you're dead and all?"

I stood up and pushed his wallet and its contents toward him. "If I didn't feel like a wanted criminal—which I no doubt am by now— I would take a walk around the block."

"That's a great idea, Leo. I don't mean around the block or anywhere outside, of course. But why don't you walk around in the front room till the food gets here?"

"Go ahead and call for the groceries, Charlie. Then take a shower and change those clothes. I'll take a walk around the front room. But when I come back, I expect you to tell me how we're going to get rid—*dispose* of John. With dignity, of course."

Charlie assumed the look of a mortician who has just been told price is no object. "Now you're talking, Leo."

I made three-and-a-half laps around the front room—not counting the extra steps it took to go around the coffee table. A lap took quite a while because I stopped to peek through the front window curtain each time to see if there were any cops about to storm the house. I couldn't be sure, but it felt as if I might be developing a twitch in my left eye.

The television sat in silence in the corner, but I resisted the temptation to turn it on. If my face was on the FBI's most wanted, I didn't want to see it. Instead, I sat on the couch across the room where I could keep an eye on the street through a tiny gap in the curtain. There wasn't an ancient *Police Gazette* magazine to thumb through like the tough guys at their hideout in the old black and white gangster movies, so I made do with the *TV Guide*. I didn't feel at all like James Cagney or George Raft. More like Stan Laurel.

Less than an hour passed before an old pickup truck screeched to a stop in front of the house. An energetic young man hopped out and grabbed a big cardboard box from the back and hurried up to the porch. Charlie met him at the door. I couldn't make out much of what was said, but I did hear my name mentioned a couple times. Never a good sign when Charlie is mentioning it to anyone with money in the conversation. I didn't have to wait long before hearing the details.

"Good news, Leo," Charlie said as he brought the box across the room, dropped it on the coffee table in front of me, and pulled out a bag of chips.

I searched through the contents. "What kind of grocery order is this? All I see are bags of chips and cookies, candy bars, a gallon of ice cream, and a quart of milk."

"Ain't it great? Don't have to cook a thing. And don't gotta pay nothin' for thirty days, except the interest."

"Not even a loaf of. . .what interest?"

"Nothing to worry about, Leo. It's all figured in with the bill."

I sank back into the sofa in a heap of despair.

Charlie tossed me a candy bar from the box followed by a bag of chips. Both bounced off my chest and onto the floor.

"I think I know how we can give John a dignified send-off," he said while he picked up the candy and chips off the floor and laid the chips in my lap. He unwrapped the candy bar and stuffed half of it in his mouth. "Make ourselves a few bucks while we're at it, too."

"Sure, Charlie. I mean, what do I have to lose at this point? My savings? My house? My freedom?"

"Don't forget the van."

Instead of saying anything, I tore open the bag of chips, crammed my mouth full, and savagely chewed them. As I swallowed, I noticed the words *Super Spicy Hot* on the bag.

Charlie understood enough body language to hand me the milk carton after seeing me turn a blazing red with my tongue sticking out and gasping for breath. It was only after three huge gulps I discovered it was buttermilk.

"Now, Leo, don't you feel better after having something to eat?"

I didn't take time to answer. I was too busy racing to the bathroom.

Once in the bathroom I ignored the disaster he had left that in when he had showered and changed clothes, and let the porcelain throne work its magic. Messy, but magic enough to make me want to keep on living.

When I came back in the living room, Charlie was finishing up the *Super Spicy Hot* chips and washing them down with the last of the buttermilk. "All right," I sank down onto the couch. "Let me hear your dignified send-off scheme."

"That's the spirit, Leo." He licked his fingers, then wiped them off on the back of what-used-to-be-my pants. "Remember me telling you about taking a stiff around to bars?"

I reached into the grocery box and fished out a candy bar. "I remember."

"Well, I got this friend tends a bar over on Sycamore. All we gotta do is find out what customer died lately."

"How do you know someone died?"

"I dunno. Folks die all the time. Why not somebody that used to drink there?"

"Sure, why not?" I carefully read the candy label to see if it had any super spicy ingredients. It didn't, so I took a bite and sank further into the cushions while Charlie babbled on.

I must have dozed off sometime during the detailed description of his friend's bar, its customers, and the selections on the jukebox.

Sometime later Charlie bounded back into the living room wearing one of his trademark smiles. "It's all set, Leo. We got our first showin' Friday night."

"But," I got to my feet and tried to shake the fuzziness out of my head. "That's two days away."

"You've been asleep, Leo, it's already Thursday morning."

I looked at the wall clock. The display glowed an impersonal 12:18 AM. I flopped back onto the coach. "My mistake. This means we're almost late, huh? What are we supposed to do till then?"

Charlie was back to the grocery box. "What we been doing, I guess. Except we'll need some more food."

I let my head fall back against the couch and stared at the ceiling for several moments. "First."

"Huh?"

"You said 'first.' What do you mean *first* showing?"

"Oh," he stuck a handful of chips in his mouth, "just a figure of sayin'."

"No, no. Not in your case. There isn't going to be any second,

70

third, or, or. . .maybe not even a first."

Chips flew out of his mouth. "How can you say that when we're so close to our dream?"

"*Your* dream, Charlie. My nightmare."

"Please, Leo, just give it a chance."

I stood my ground. "No way. I've had enough."

He carefully folded the bag of chips like closing a King James Version of the Good Book, and took on the air of a mortician who has just been accused of overcharging for a casket. "Okay, Leo," he said as he collapsed onto the couch next to me. "I see the problem. I should've seen it earlier."

"About time."

"I get cranky myself when I don't eat right. Forget about John for a while."

"His sister said his name was Butch."

"Aw, that was probably a nickname. Besides, he'll always be 'John' to us. What would you like to eat, Leo? I mean a *real* meal."

Charlie could be so disarmingly sincere at times. I allowed myself a little wishful dreaming. "Fried chicken, corn on the cob, mashed potatoes and gravy."

"Let me get it for you, Leo. Please?" His sincerity level was on high.

"No."

"C'mon, Leo. Why not?"

"Because every time you do something for me, it ends up to be something *to* me."

He hung his head and clutched the bag of chips to his chest. "Please?" he whispered.

"All right, Charlie. Go ahead and get me some fried chicken. You

71

might even be right about me needing a good meal."

"Now you're talking." He jumped up and rushed toward the kitchen phone. A minute later he stuck his head around the counter as far as the phone cord would reach. "Hey Leo, what's your credit card number?"

There was nothing else to do but give him the number. I already had my mind set on some fried chicken. Extra crispy.

After the chicken dinner arrived and I had eaten my fill, I actually did feel better. The fact Charlie had ordered another bucket of chicken and two orders of fries for himself didn't even bother me.

The rest of the day crawled along with nap breaks, another grocery delivery from Charlie's friend, and countless laps around the living room.

Friday arrived with a dreary rain which letup before noon, but the dreariness continued to drape the world. Except for Charlie's world, of course. It never rained there. Seems like any rain headed for his world somehow got dumped in mine instead. And I didn't have long to wait for another downpour.

The back door slammed as Charlie came in. He flopped down on the couch between me and the most recently delivered box of goodies. "We might have a little problem with John, Leo."

"Are you talking about the little problem we've *been* having, or have you discovered a new little problem?"

All I heard was a mumble as he stuffed his mouth with chips, so I wasn't sure if he meant we had a new problem, or he was just now realizing we've had a problem. It became clear after he swallowed some of the chips and managed a muffled, "The van smells."

I had completely forgotten about John's odor situation. With the recent rain and warm temps, the inside of the van must be enough to gag a road kill collector. Not only inside the van, but the entire neighborhood would soon share this little problem. Thankfully, the van windows were closed.

"Don't worry, Leo. Think I fixed it. I opened the doors in the van to air it out. Even poured some of your aftershave lotion in there. I'll check again in about an hour to see if it worked."

"My neighbors, Charlie." I jumped up and looked out through the drapes. "They're going to smell that. Then they're going to come over here to complain. But I won't answer the door. So they'll call the police. Then the police will come and knock on the door. But I still won't open the door. And when that happens, *they* know how to open doors."

"But we won't be here, Leo. A few more hours we'll be showing John down at the bar."

"Not with that smell, we won't." I began to pace back and forth in front of the window—peeking out through the drapes on each pass.

"Maybe we can get rid of it the way they do at the mortuary. I watched my friend do that stuff and it didn't look too hard."

"Stop right there, Charlie. We are not going to do anything of the sordid. . .sort."

"How about we take a drive in the country with the windows open and air John out."

"You don't understand. The smell isn't on John, it's *coming* from him."

"Well, maybe we'll run over a skunk or something."

There was no doubt in my mind by this time. I had definitely developed a twitch in my left eye. It seemed to grow more pronounced whenever he offered one of his solutions to our increasing number of *little* problems.

I stopped pacing and fell back onto the couch. As soon as my breathing slowed to a more normal rhythm, I actually felt more in control of things. It wasn't clear whether I was thinking more coherently, or simply losing what was left of my mind and falling deeper into Charlie's world. Either way the words came out in an even flow, "We have reached the point of no return. Our. . .my back is against the wall, and I have a suggestion."

He looked at me with the same expression as a Labrador Retriever when you make a sound like a kitten.

"The time has come when we have no choice but to get rid, uh, that would be *dispose* of John. Now, after giving the matter very little thought, I think the thing to do is to take him to that bar tonight, keep the van closed up tight, and get as much money as we can from the showing. Then we use the money to take care of him. What do you think?"

He looked like the Lab when you pull out your car keys.

"Really, Leo?" He jumped off the couch and scattered most of his chips. But he maintained a grip on his soda, which fizzed all over the coffee table and carpet. "That's great." He strode back and forth in front of the couch several times before he sat back down on the edge of the couch and picked up the half-empty bag of chips.

"I'm glad you see it my way, Charlie. Now we can concentrate on putting John out of our life. For good. Right?"

The Lab just watched you use his water dish you call the commode.

It took him several moments to recover, but he was surprisingly calm and coherent as he sank back into the cushions. "Maybe you're right, Leo. It might be his time to go."

I went and did it to myself again. I stepped right up to the plate and took a swing at the high and outside by asking, "What do you suggest?"

He answered in a soft voice, "Cremation." He picked a single chip out of the crumpled bag and held it up to the light and studied it while he waited for me to say something. I refused to rise to the bait. He placed the chip in his mouth and delicately chewed on it until it stopped crunching. He then followed that display with a large handful of chips and considerably less delicate chewing.

I finally gave in. "All right, Charlie. How are we going to get John cremated without all the legal paperwork those cremation places ask for? Or by spending a load of cash?"

"I got this friend," he swallowed the chips, "got a pizza place. We take John in after closing time, use the oven, then put the ashes in a pizza box."

"Pizza ovens aren't big enough for a body."

"Well, we could—"

"Don't even say it. Besides, they don't get hot enough to cremate a body."

Charlie looked defeated. Almost. He went into one of his deep-thinking moods. The routine varied with the seriousness of the situation. In this case, it consisted of striding back and forth several times with his hands clasped behind his back while slightly bent over at the waist. Then an abrupt stop, straightening up, and stabbing his finger in the air at imaginary balloons for a full minute. A momentary freeze in the action, a few more strides, and another stop with a frenzied announcement.

"Okay," he said with his arms spread wide, "we go to a funeral while everybody's inside. Then we put John in the hearse, see?"

All I could take in from that point on was *blah, blah, blah.*

He finally noticed my blank look, so he eased up to the edge of the couch and patiently tried to clarify the *blah, blah, blah*. "We go to some funeral while all the folks are still inside, see? Then we put John inside the hearse, in front of where the casket is gonna be. See?"

"I see what you're saying, Charlie, but what happens when they see him laying back there?"

"Nothin'." It's hard to imagine how a man with a mouthful of super spicy hot chips can grin from ear to ear. But there it was.

"Here's how it is, Leo. Pallbearers don't look inside the hearse. They just slide the casket in looking down at the ground and sad and all. Then, when they get to the grave they do the same thing, only in the other direction."

"How about the driver who closes the back door to the hearse? How can he help but see John?"

"That's the best part. We *want* him to see John. See?"

"Not quite," was all I could come up with.

He took a deep breath, sip of the soda, another handful of chips, and tried to explain to me the extended translation of *blah, blah, blah*. "The driver, you see, is gonna think John must've fell outta the casket somehow. Now, he don't wanna look bad to his boss by lettin' something like that happen in his hearse, see? So, he finds a way to sneak John under the casket just before they lower it, say some prayers, then cover it all up."

"Charlie, one of us has lost it."

"What do you mean, Leo? Here's the solution we've been looking for. It's got everything we wanted. Some money from the showin', John's gone where nobody will ever find him, and he's laid to rest with dignity."

"Where's the dignity in all that?"

"Leo, you haven't been paying attention. Funeral, pallbearers, flowers, music, prayers. Even a casket. How do you get more dignified than all that?"

"But John isn't even *in* the casket."

"He don't know that."

All I could do was stare at the floor and shake my head.

"Are you more against the idea, Leo, or against giving John a dignified send away? Remember, we're the only family he's got."

That brought me around. "We are *not* the only family he's got." I jumped up from the couch and began to stomp around the room with my voice rising with every question I shot at him. "Remember his sister? The one with the two unsmiling guys who look like they spend all their spare time in a boxing ring? With all this thought about John we've neglected to think about her. And them. He might have other family, too. What if he has a wife? Kids?"

Charlie's exuberance waned. In a somber voice he said, "You're right, Leo. They should be a part of this. No reason we should have to pay for it all."

"That isn't the point, Charlie." I settled down on the edge of the couch and tried my best to pry open a small crack in his anti-reality shield. "His family, his *real* family should decide how to get rid. . .lay him to rest. Can't you see that?"

He quietly toyed with the chip between his thumb and forefinger for a moment or two, then filled his hand with chips from the crumpled bag and stuffed them in his mouth. After chewing them down to a manageable pulp he mumbled something incoherent. I waited till he washed it all down with the last of his soda and caught his breath.

He wiped his mouth with the back of his hand, belched, and said, "I got a question."

"You mean before you say something stupid, or after?"

"You know, Leo, sometimes you hurt my feelings."

"I'm sorry. I only do it because you sometimes wreck my entire life."

There was a momentary pause while he brushed some chip crumbs off his shirt. "I understand your apology. But how you gonna get John's family in on all this?"

Before I could come back with a snappy answer, it dawned on me I had no earthly idea how to contact John's family. Or even who his family was, for that matter. All I could do was sit there with my mouth half-open and stare at him. The way I normally did whenever Charlie said anything even remotely related to some kind of logic.

He looked at me with his head cocked to one side for a moment. "Did you want to say something, Leo?"

All I could do was slowly shake my head. With my mouth half-open.

"Okay. If you want John's family to know where he's at, here's how we can do it."

We had come full circle back to the *we* part. But by now I had spent entirely too much time in his world to be shocked or surprised by anything he had to say. I thought.

"All we got to do is take John around on showings. Sooner or after, his other family has got to spot him. Then they can make up a mind if they want a better send-away then what we can give him."

I had trouble closing my mouth, but finally managed to regain my muscle control. "We can't just drive John around indefinitely."

"Yeah, I know. The van's gonna need gas. But the first showin's gonna bring in cash for that."

"What about the odor?"

"We'll get used to it."

"No, Charlie. *I* will not get used to it, and the people viewing John will not get used to it."

He slowly got up and stood looking up at the ceiling with his feet apart, right elbow cradled in his left hand, and stroked his chin with his right hand as if he had a beard.

As much as I enjoyed the silence, I simply had to ask, "Now what?"

Without taking his eyes off the ceiling, he held up the index finger of his right hand for a moment or two. Then, like a psychic announcing the presence of a dearly departed relative to a gullible client, said, "I have the answer."

"I'm afraid to ask to which question."

"The stink question, Leo," he said as he came out of his trance and looked at me like I hadn't been paying enough attention to him. "We can even make a little extra money on the side with this."

"Let's start with the answer before we engage in any more of your schemes."

He put on his disarming grin that never failed to send shivers up and down my spine. "Limburger."

"Excuse me?"

"The cheese. Limburger cheese. My friend at the grocery store sells it."

"Oh, for crying out loud, Charlie. Not even Limburger cheese can out-smell John at this point."

"It could if we put enough of it around him. Besides, we're running out of food anyway. And we'll have to have some crackers."

"How did this all come down to crackers?"

"The money next to the side, like I said. With all that cheese smell, folks are gonna get a little hungry. 'Specially after drinking like they do in the bar and all. We sell the lookers some cheese 'n' crackers after they pass by Mike."

"Who's Mike?"

"Mike's the dead guy that John's gonna pretend to be."

"I see. Think John can pull it off?"

"Sure he can. He's a natural."

I shook my head. "How could I have not seen something so obvious?"

"You just gotta learn to use your 'magination, Leo. It'll come to you after a time or two."

"Maybe I'll get some of that kind of imagination about the time you get sarcasm."

"You trying to hurt my feelings again, Leo?"

"No, Charlie. Just trying to point out some obvious facts of life."

"Oh. Okay then." He walked toward the kitchen phone. "I'll go ahead and order some more food and the Limburger cheese. Should I go ahead and get the crackers?"

"Why not." Then I had a thought. "Is that stuff going to get here before we have to leave for the bar showing?"

"Sure. I'll just have 'em put it on a rush order. Costs a little more, but it'll be here."

"Fine. What's a little more money on the old credit card?" I leaned back into the couch cushions and quickly fell into a fitful sleep.

I had a dream someone was knocking on the front door. I was yelling at whoever was there to go away. The knocking got louder and louder until it woke me up. The banging at the door didn't go away, though.

Charlie hollered out from the bathroom, "Leo, can you get that? Kinda busy here."

I pulled myself up from the couch and groggily headed for the door, wiping the sleep from my eyes. All the events from the past few days were beginning to catch up with me. I swung the door open and stood face-to-face with a short man dressed in khaki pants and a casual shirt. The official-looking ID card pinned to his shirt did not look casual, though. It had a large city emblem with the guy's picture, and the words *Code Enforcement*. He was not smiling.

"I'm here about the van in your back yard, sir."

My Adam's apple struggled with an uncontrollable urge to swallow, while my mind silently shrieked, *For god's sake don't just stand here trying to swallow, say something.* I finally managed to blurt out, "V. . .van?"

"Yes, sir. One of your neighbors alerted us."

By *us*, I assumed he meant the entire city, police department, FBI, CIA, and every other law enforcement agency in the country. In a way, I felt relieved. The pressure was off. Maybe I could now at least get a decent night's sleep in the slammer. I would deal with my conscience later.

After waiting a respectful interval for me to say something, but hearing nothing coming out of my open mouth, the officer said, "This is just a warning, but if you don't move that van, I'll have to issue a citation for parking on an unapproved surface."

My mouth fell open even more as I simply stared at him. God only knows what I must have looked like.

The enforcer obviously took that look as insolence as his eye's narrowed and returned my stare. But in a more steely manner. "I can assure you, *sir*, this is not a matter to mock. The city is very serious about enforcing parking codes. So serious, I'm going to make a special visit here tomorrow to see if your attitude has changed and that you have complied with the code. *Sir*."

With that, he spun around and stomped off to the car at the curb. It was a plain sedan with the city emblem on the door above the large letters: *CODE ENFORCEMENT*. Things had taken a definite turn for the worse.

The groceries were delivered shortly after my wake-up call. Charlie deftly signed my name to the bill and emptied the groceries on the coffee table. He tossed the empty box in the corner with the others. "I'll take those out later."

Even through the heavy foil wrappers, I could smell the Limburger. It was like being up close and personal with John.

Charlie, of course, was unaffected by the stench and dove into the pile to retrieve a bag of chips and a carton of buttermilk. "Here's something for you, Leo," he said as he handed me a small piece of paper with numbers scribbled on it.

"What's this?"

"Prices," he answered while he ripped open the chips and plopped down on the couch. "I figured out what we can charge for the cheese 'n' crackers."

I looked at all the numbers randomly scattered at all angles on the paper. "Which one?"

"The ones circled."

"Most *all* of them are circled."

He took a drink of the buttermilk. "Oh, yeah. The ones in a circle with a line under them."

I looked again and found the circle with the underlined numbers, *2/1-2/2-1/0-1/1-0/1-0/2.*

"These numbers supposed to mean something to anyone besides you?"

He gave me one of his *I-can't-believe-you-don't-understand* looks. "It's really simple, Leo."

"Go slow for me."

"Okay. The first number means two cracker squares and the second number means one small slice of cheese." He paused while he shoved some chips into his mouth and chewed with slow deliberation while he waited for me to catch up.

"A little faster," I said. "I'll try to keep up."

"If you say so." He took a swallow of buttermilk and went on. "The second number two and the two after that means two crackers and two slices of cheese. The number one after that—"

"Stop. It can be for whatever you want, Charlie. You can charge whatever you want. You can even keep the money from whatever you sell. All I want is an end to this nightmare."

He seemed confused by my tone of voice, and the good news about keeping all the proceeds from his latest brainstorm. He finally settled the matter on the side of the good news with a big grin and filled his mouth with a fresh load of chips.

I made a trip into the bathroom and splashed some cool water on my face. As I toweled off I cringed at my haggard reflection. Staring back at me was the Hollywood stereotype of a horror movie undertaker. Oddly enough, it didn't shock me. It only confirmed my suspicions.

The time finally dragged around to zero hour. Charlie unwrapped about half the Limburger cheese and put it around John. The rest of it went into a small cardboard box with the crackers. He was more excited than a kid on the last day of school. Or a parent on the *first* day of school.

"C'mon, Leo. Don't want to be late for our first showin'."

I didn't even try to correct him about this being our *only* showing. As I passed by my sideways storm door, now forever a part of the passenger side of the van, I looked in at John. Charlie had covered him up again with my blanket. It had been my favorite. Green, with pictures of Leprechauns and little pots of gold. The box of cheese and crackers sat on top of the blanket to keep it from blowing off while we drove with the windows down.

I settled into the wobbly passenger seat and buckled up. Charlie jumped in behind the wheel and turned the key. The van wheezed its way up to an imitation of life. Then he stomped on the gas and made a four-inch-deep furrow in the wet ground on our way out. I wasn't sure if I should be upset over the trench in my back yard, or amazed the van had the power to create it. I decided to just sit and stare out at the passing scenery like a depressed undertaker who has just heard about another increased life expectancy in the world.

It turned out Sycamore Street was located in the part of town with narrow streets and minimal upkeep. I felt each jarring impact with the endless potholes would be the van's last, but it kept rattling along until we reached *The Starlight Lounge*. The sun was giving up its last bit of light from the day shift, which meant a dark ride back home.

The lounge sat back from the blacktop by about five or six feet, and was closely flanked by unpainted houses with bed sheets for curtains. There was no curb, no sidewalk, or anything green growing in the packed dirt surrounding the lounge or the nearby houses. The lounge door was open and loud music, laughter, and colored beer sign lights spilled out through a smoky haze from the interior. But no outside lights advertised the festivities within.

Sycamore dead-ended a few yards beyond, and Charlie managed to turn the van around without hitting one of the numerous cars and pickups parked willy-nilly along the street and in the yards. Judging from the looks of the vehicles, the local hardware stores no doubt had a tough time keeping wire and duct tape in stock.

The end of Sycamore looked like the end of everything I knew as normal.

Charlie stopped the van in front with my side facing the open door. "C'mon in," he said. "Meet some of the folks."

"If it's all the same, I'll wait here till this is all over."

"Whatever you say, Leo. I'll just tell everybody you're too grieved to come in."

I didn't have long to grieve alone before some of the lounge patrons began to trickle out and pay their respects to a departed buddy.

The first mourner was a lady well past middle age with a highball glass in one hand. She wore a flowered dress with a long string of pearls around her neck. Brilliant red lipstick went far beyond the outline of her thin lips, but perfectly matched the large dangling earrings that stretched her earlobes to the snapping point. She made her way on wobbly high heels directly toward me and steadied herself with her free hand on the van above my head. She stuck her head inside and spilled most of her whiskey sour in my lap. "I'm so sorry for your loss," she slurred. "I can see the family resemblance in your eyes. Be strong."

At that, she spilled the rest of her drink on me as she pushed herself away from the van and staggered back inside.

Charlie came out and climbed into the back, adjusted my blanket around John's head for a more shadowy view, and retrieved the cheese and crackers. Someone inside called his name, so he got out and dropped the box onto my lap on his way back in.

The next customer looked like a lumberjack with a miniature beer bottle in his hand. It wasn't until he got closer I realized it was a regular beer bottle, but the huge size of his hand made it look tiny. He stopped at the front of the van for a moment, took a drink of the beer, and stood looking up at the sky. I saw a tear run down his left cheek. A moment later he lowered his head and wiped his nose with the back of his hand and walked toward the side of the van. As he was passing by me he glanced down and saw the box of cheese and crackers in my lap. He stopped and swayed like a tall oak in the wind. "You got some kind of nerve to sit there and eat at a time like this. How the hell can you be so disrespectful?"

A lot of "uh, uh, uhs" came out of my mouth before I finally came up with, "Mike made me promise to put on some weight before he died."

The big man hesitated for several of my pounding heartbeats, then said, "Yeah, that sounds like Ol' Mike." He loudly sniffed and returned inside without even looking at Ol' Mike. Or John.

More people came out in two's and three's, or singly. Some talked low to each other, while others simply looked at John, or Mike, in silence, took a drink or two from their glass or bottle, then went back inside. All things considered, the evening was going pretty well.

By now the only light on the street came from inside the bar, but Charlie had still not come back out. I wasn't sure if that was a good thing or not. But he had been right about one thing, I was getting used to the Limburger smell and hardly noticed John's odor at all. The box of cheese sitting under my nose may have had something to do with it.

A young blond woman with a ponytail wearing a pair of tight-fitting jeans, cowboy boots, and a low-cut peasant blouse charged out with a bottle of beer in her hand. A tattoo on the left side of her ample chest said "Sweet," while one on the right said "Sour." A dark haired woman was trying to hold her back, but the blond squirmed free and stumbled on toward the van—swearing and crying at the same time. "Mike, you sonuvabitch. Think dyin's better than marryin' me?"

At first I thought she was yelling at me instead of at John, or Mike. It made no difference. She almost hit me when she threw her beer bottle at the van. The other woman grabbed her arm before she could get any closer, pushed her into a nearby car, and leaned against the door to keep her from getting back out. She was evidently too drunk to realize the car had a door on the other side.

As the excitement died down, the more reserved crowd took over again. This time, though, I began to notice some of the folks on a return visit. They usually had one or two others with them and did a lot of pointing at John, or Mike, and talking in low tones. I strained to hear what they were saying without being too obvious. The words and phrases I managed to pick up on raised goose bumps on my arms and sent a chill up and down my spine.

What I heard most often were negative words and phrases.

"Not. . ."

"Couldn't be."

"No way. . ."

"He didn't. . ."

"The Mike I knew wasn't. . ."

"No chance in hell."

Even in the dark, I began to suspect John's impersonation wasn't going so well.

My suspicion was confirmed a few minutes later when Charlie came out at a fast walk, got in behind the wheel, and began to search through his pockets. Before I could ask him to take the cheese and crackers out of my lap, he said, "My friend the bartender said some of the folks don't think John is Mike. He figures the customer's always right, so he decided not to give us any money this time. We might as well go back home."

By now a crowd was beginning to gather between the lounge and the van as more and more people came out to look at John, but fewer and fewer of them went back inside. Except for the ones with an empty glass or bottle. They went back in for a refill and returned a couple minutes later. Usually with one or two others.

The negative conversations seemed to be increasing. And louder.

Charlie was oblivious to it all as he kept searching for something in his pockets.

Cigarette lighters and matches flared in the crowd as the heavy smokers fired up continuously, and others were lighting matches in an attempt to see their dearly departed buddy better.

When Doctor Frankenstein looked through one of the castle windows at the approaching villagers with their pitchforks and torches, he must've thought the same thing going through my mind. *Nothing good is likely to come of this.*

"Did you sell much cheese and crackers?"

I turned my attention back to Charlie. "Forget the cheese. What are you looking for? Let's get out of here."

"I was hoping those sales would bring in a few bucks."

"Stop talking, Charlie. Let's go!"

"Can't find the keys."

The crowd kept growing and rumbling louder.

"They're in the ignition, you dummy."

"Aw, Leo. You don't have to talk to me like that."

"Okay. Sorry. Would you get us out of here? Now, please?"

"Sure. But you don't have to yell so loud."

I saw the top of the lumberjack as he made a path through the crowd toward the van. He was like a shark's fin cutting through the water. And there was nothing slowing him down.

Charlie stomped the accelerator to the floorboard a few times and turned the key. The engine made sounds like a teenager fighting to stay asleep while someone is trying to wake him.

The crowd's murmurs grew into angry shouts. "Who they think we are, anyway?"

"Disrespectful of the dead."

"What would Mike's mother say?"

"We ain't gonna let 'em get away with this, are we?"

Charlie stomped a few more times. The engine finally came awake with a weak cough and a groan.

"Good going, Charlie. Now get us out of here."

"Just need to adjust the mirror."

"Later. Do it later. Just *go*."

The van performed as usual in our getaway. Like a long freight train pulling out of the yards. Slow, but steady. I silently cursed the slowness, but gave thanks for the steady part.

The last thing I could make out in the darkness through the rear view mirror was several people jumping into nearby cars and pickups. It didn't appear they were waiting for their vehicles to warm up either before they spun tires and fell in behind us.

The last voice I could make out was, "Mike, you sonuvabitch. If you think I'm gonna let you rest in peace you're crazy."

As bad as Sycamore Street was, it actually worked in our favor. With parked vehicles on both sides it was too narrow for anyone to pass us as long as we stayed in the center. The convoy of drunken villagers snaked bumper-to-bumper behind us. Each vehicle kept trying to pass the one in front—first on the right, then on the left.

Unfortunately, I could see a block or two away our advantage disappeared as the neighborhood improved enough for street lights, and Sycamore got wider. I frantically began to look for an escape route.

Besides the potholes, the street was littered with parked cars and pickups. Some on the side, some in yards, some on cinder blocks. But I spotted an open space between two houses that looked big enough for the van.

By this time even Charlie had figured out things hadn't gone quite as planned. He barely hesitated when I screamed, "Turn left. Now!"

The van performed like a well-trained circus dog and abruptly left the street, scraped between two houses, and made a right down an alley.

Unfortunately, my storm door, the refrigerator box casket, and John did not. All three continued on their way down Sycamore and stopped in the middle of the street. With John on top.

The car immediately behind us was taken by surprise with the sudden tactic. The sight of John laying in the middle of the street also took the driver by surprise. Instead of trying to follow us he slammed on the brakes to keep from running over John. This sudden move also took several drivers behind him by surprise.

I caught sight of only the first car making contact with the one in front of it through the rear view mirror. But I had no trouble visualizing what several tipsy drivers following too close to the car in front of them were doing when the first one made a sudden stop.

Charlie turned right down the alley and took a zig-zag course of side streets back to the house. He said only one thing on the way back. "You got any cheese an' crackers left?"

I spent the rest of the night curled up in the fetal position on the couch. My eyes wide open. And my teeth clenched.

A little before noon, Charlie came into the front room munching on Limburger and crackers. "The van's got a flat. I'm gonna walk over to my friend's place and see if he's got a spare we can borrow."

"Don't bother." I had graduated from the fetal position to a dejected slouch by then. "I don't have any money for gas anyway."

"Oh," he shoved the last of his cracker into his mouth and mumbled, "it's no bother. Want me to call the store for anything before I go?"

"Maybe later."

"You sure? You ain't had anything to eat since yesterday."

"I'm fine. I'll just have a few of those leftover crackers."

"That was the last one."

"Last of the Limburger, too, I hope?"

"Uh huh. Want me to get some more?"

"No, that's all right. The way it is now, I'll probably smell the stuff in the house for a month."

Charlie picked up an empty grocery box and tossed it on top of the others. "I'll take those out in a little while." Then he looked at me with one of his dog-begging-at-the-table expressions.

"If I call for some groceries now, they could be here about the time I get back."

"Why not." I didn't feel like trying to explain to him about the ill-health of my credit card.

"Great. Anything special you want?"

I just shook my head.

He rushed into the kitchen to downgrade my credit card's condition to critical.

In a few minutes he came back out and bounded out the door. "I'll be back in a few minutes."

It would make no difference how long before he got back. His appetite would grow enough by then to make his grocer friend celebrate, buy a new delivery truck, and order more empty boxes.

I pulled the drape open a slit and watched him saunter down the walk. Not a care in the world. But being around him is like being in an earthquake while in the middle of a cloud of ravenous mosquitos.

My reverie was interrupted when I saw a nondescript sedan pull up at the curb. Two men in suits got out, walked to the front door, and knocked. It was one of those firm kind of knocks. Not disrespectful or obnoxious, but firm. With confident authority. The kind of authority that comes with carrying a badge and a gun.

My instinct screamed at me to run to the bedroom and hide under my bed. But then my ragged intellect reminded me the police know how to open doors that people don't open for them. I put on my best casual look and opened the door. Even at that, I probably looked like a startled Chihuahua.

The shorter of the two spoke first. "Leo Walker? We're from homicide. Like to ask you a few questions."

I hadn't even opened my mouth and he already knew who I was. Obviously, lying was out of the question from this point on. My only chance would be an evasive response. "Uh, uh?"

He already had a thin wallet open to reveal a police I.D. card on one side, and a heavy looking badge on the opposite side. When he introduced himself and his partner, the only names ringing in my head were Sergeant Joe Friday and Partner. He didn't show me his gun and I didn't ask to see it.

"Yes, sir. I'm Leo. Leo Walker. That's my real name."

"Did you drive your van anywhere last night?"

"My van?"

Officer Partner held a bent-up license plate in front of my face. "We found this a couple blocks from *The Starlight Lounge* this morning. It belongs to a van recently purchased by you."

"Oh, my van. I remember now." How could they *know* all this? "Uh, no. I didn't drive it. Anywhere. Last night."

Detective Friday asked, "Do you know where it is right now, Mister Walker?"

"Uh, well. . ."

"Doesn't have to be exact. Within a block or so would be okay."

"Last," I cleared my throat and swallowed hard, "last time I remember, it was in the back yard."

"Mind if we come in? And could I take a look at your van?"

"Of course. That is, I mean, I don't mind. Mi casa, your castle. And, uh, look at the van. You can go through the house to the back yard where the van is. There's nothing in it, though. Not even. . . Nothing."

Detective Friday made his way through the house to the back yard. I eased down onto the couch while Officer Partner stood and stared at me. He reminded me of those Easter Island statues. But with a body. And less emotion.

After several uncomfortable minutes, Detective Friday returned and went into a hushed conversation with his partner on the other side of the room. After much head shaking and nodding, Officer Partner sat on the arm of the couch to my right. He placed his left hand on the couch behind my head. Friday sat next to me on my left.

"You know why we're here, don't you Mister Walker?"

He obviously knew more than I did. But I couldn't decide whether to nod or shake my head. It probably ended up looking like my head was making a shaky circle.

"Don't act stupid," Officer Partner said. "It's about the body you threw out of your van last night." He sniffed and looked around before adding, "Maybe about another dead body you've got around here, too."

I somehow managed to find enough of my voice to squeak out, "That's cheese. And he fell out. Sir."

"Yeah, sure," he said. "And you didn't drive your van last night, either. So how do you know the body fell out, or got thrown out?"

My mouth opened half-way, but then all my communication methods froze. Except for blinking like an out of control lighthouse on steroids.

Officer Partner leaned close to my face. He must have shaved earlier that morning, but a dark stubble was already pushing out. He probably didn't even need a gun. Breath mints, maybe.

"So which is it, Walker, did the stiff fall out or did you throw it out?"

My mouth felt like I had been chewing on a handful of cinnamon between two crackers. Swallowing was out of the question. As was any elusive answer to the question. All I could do was look from one cop to the other and make sounds like a choking crow.

Before Officer Partner could demand another impossible response from me, the front door suddenly banged open and a tire rolled into the front room. With Charlie right behind it.

Both cops were instantly on their feet. Detective Friday leapt up with his gun pointed at Charlie and shouted, "On the floor! On the floor!"

As it turned out, Officer Partner *did* have a gun. He whipped it out and pointed it at me while his eyes darted from Charlie, to Friday, then back at me. I quit trying to caw.

Charlie dropped to the floor—on his back with his hands folded over his chest. The tire wobbled its way into the next room and crashed into something, followed by the sound of something else crashing to the floor. "I didn't steal it, honest. Friend of mine loaned it to me."

Detective Friday put his gun back under his jacket. "And you must be Charlie?"

"Yes, sir," he answered as he continued to stare at the ceiling. "Charlie Bernard."

I couldn't understand why he kept asking questions when he already knew the answers.

Officer Partner's gun disappeared as abruptly as it had appeared. "Get off the floor and sit over here next to your friend."

Everyone took his place on the couch. Charlie and I were

sandwiched between the two cops with our hands in our laps like two schoolboys about to get a lecture before the real punishment comes.

Friday crossed his left leg over his right knee and rested his right arm behind me on the back of the couch. "I think we can clear all this up in no time if you'll just be honest. Will you do that for me, Mister Walker? And may I call you 'Leo?'"

I nodded my consent twice for both questions.

"Good. Now it *was* you in the van at *The Starlight Lounge* last night, wasn't it, Leo?"

And yet another question he already knew the answer to. All I could do was nod again. I was beginning to feel like a bobble head.

"That was a pretty creative idea you boys came up with. Who was the corpse?"

I felt like a contestant on a game show who was confident he had the right answer that stumped the others. "Butch."

But at the same time Charlie answered just as confidently, "John."

The cops glanced at each other, then back at me. Friday's sincere mood wavered, but quickly returned. Officer Partner's stony glare remained unchanged.

"Which is it, Leo?" Friday asked.

"Uh, kinda both, but informal. Not like a formal name on a birth certificate, or on your driver's license. We didn't know him till after he got dead. His sister called him 'Butch.'"

"So, you're acquainted with the family?"

"No. And we don't really *know* her. We just kinda met in passing. Not really a regular *met*, either. More like a, a—"

The doorbell saved me from more stammering.

"You expecting someone, Leo?"

I expected him to answer his own question like he had been doing, but after an uncomfortable pause, Charlie said, "I'll get it. It's probably the groceries."

He tried to get up, but Officer Partner pushed him back onto the couch. The cops exchanged another look, then Friday nodded.

Officer Partner walked with Charlie and stood out of sight as Charlie opened the door. He signed the receipt, took the box, and closed the door. Partner made a quick, but thorough, inspection of the contents before a quick nod indicated his okay of the situation.

Charlie set the box on the coffee table, as usual, and took a bag of chips out, as usual. Partner grabbed the bag out of his hand and tossed it back into the box, guided him firmly back onto the couch, and returned to his perch next to him on the arm.

Detective Friday continued his efforts to clear things up. "So, your friend calls the deceased, 'John,' and you and the sister-you-don't-know call him 'Butch.' How did all that come about?"

"Well, when we first got Butch, Charlie's friend said he was a John Doe, so that's what we called him till we heard his sister say his name was Butch."

"I see. Who is Charlie's friend?"

"He used to work nights at the city morgue, but he's in jail now."

Friday uncrossed his legs and scooted up to the edge of the couch. But it was Partner who asked, "And this guy just gave you a corpse from the morgue? Or did you take it when he wasn't looking?"

"Actually," I turned back to Friday, "neither one. He loaned Butch to us. But his name was John at the time."

"It might help in clearing things up, Leo, if we knew the morgue worker's name."

I shrugged and gave my best honest-to-God-I-don't-know look. Charlie spoke up. "Fred."

Friday looked at him. "Does he have a last name?"

"I'm sure he does."

"Is this your way of saying you don't know what it is?"

"No. I just don't know his last name."

Friday started to say something, but changed his mind. He pulled out his cell phone as he got up and walked to the kitchen. "Keep an eye on these two while I make a call."

Even though he hadn't been looking at anyone in particular, I was pretty sure who he was talking to. Charlie, however, wasn't. He answered with a cheery, "No problem, sir."

Officer Partner firmly gripped his shoulder. "Shut up."

Several minutes later Friday came back in and sat next to me. He looked at me for a moment, then resumed his relaxed position with his left leg crossed over his right knee, and his right arm on the back of the couch behind me. "Just what made you think you could pass off this John Doe as somebody named Mike at *The Starlight Lounge*?"

There was no doubt in my mind he knew the answer to this question, but I answered it anyway. "Charlie."

He nodded. "The bartender said he was an odd duck." He was about to say something else when the doorbell rang again. All three of us looked at Charlie, who looked back at each of us and merely shrugged.

"See who it is, Leo," Friday said.

Officer Partner accompanied me as he had with Charlie and stood out of sight as I opened the door and stood face to face with the city code enforcement enforcer.

"Evidently, you did not take me serious enough about moving your van yesterday, Mister Walker." His thin lips stretched into a sneer as he pulled out what looked like a receipt book, except it had the city's logo on the cover. He flipped through several pink and blue pages until he came to a white one. "As a city official, I'm going to write you a citation that gives you forty-eight hours to move that vehicle off the grass and onto a city approved surface." He took a pen from his pocket and made an exaggerated motion of clicking it with his thumb. "If you don't move it by then, Mister Walker, the city will send a tow truck around and move it for you. Then you'll have to pay a fine, pick your van up at the auto pound, pay the towing charge, plus storage fees. Now is *that* serious enough for you?"

Words seemed to be caught crosswise in my throat. Officer Partner's words, on the other hand, were not. He stepped out from behind the door and held his I.D. wallet an inch from the code enforcer's nose. "That van is being held as evidence. Now leave."

Officer Partner suddenly became my hero. Sort of. That is, until he slammed the door in the code enforcer's face and turned to me with the same tone of voice, "Get back on the couch."

Friday welcomed me back to the couch with an observation and another question. "You seem to be pretty popular, Leo. Expecting anyone else for a while?"

I immediately answered, "No, sir," and silently prayed I hadn't lied.

"Good." He got off the couch and stretched. "A team of investigators will be here in a few minutes to go over your van. They also need to take a look around in your house. You don't mind do you, Leo?"

"Uh, well. . . Is it really necessary for them to snoop around, uh, investigate in here?"

"It's as much for your protection as it is to clear things up for the district attorney. Of course, I could always get a search warrant, but it looks better if you cooperate. You can see that can't you, Leo?"

"Oh, sure." I lied. I could see less and less the longer this thing wore on.

"Fine. Now you boys sit back and relax while my partner and I have a little discussion."

Friday and Partner walked to the other side of the room and went into another one of their hushed conversations. But try as I might, there was no way I could relax. Charlie had no problem with it, though. He stretched his legs out, clasped his hands behind his head, and closed his eyes. I fully expected him to start snoring any minute.

Five men and a dog arrived within a half-hour. I had no idea what they were investigating, but I stayed in my cooperative mode and didn't ask. Detective Friday had a conversation with them before two members went out through the back door to the van, while the others began to snoop and sniff around inside. He then joined me back on the couch. Officer Partner had evidently found something else to do more in keeping with his jovial personality.

"This," Friday said, indicating the investigators, "will take a couple of hours. During that time, we could make a little more detailed account of events that have led up to where we are now. Would you be interested in doing that for me, Leo?"

He was beginning to sound like Charlie's sincerity. All those we's, and ending up with Leo. Out of habit I nodded. I almost said *I do*, but Officer Partner had returned with something in his hand. The *I do* sounded too much like a wedding ceremony response, and I didn't want him to think I was trying to be funny.

The thing in Partner's hand turned out to be a voice recorder, which he placed on the coffee table in front of me. He then faced Charlie. "On your feet. You and me are going to the kitchen."

The word kitchen rang a bell in Charlie's head and he automatically reached for the box of snacks on the coffee table to take with him. Partner was about to grab him by the collar, but Friday smiled. "It's okay. Maybe it'll keep him out of trouble until we're gone."

After they had left the room Friday became serious. "Now Leo, I want you to understand you're not being accused of anything right now. But there have been laws broken and you may be charged with one or more of them at the end of this investigation. I have to follow some basic procedures here. The first thing I want to do is make sure you understand your rights before you make an official statement, okay?"

Before I could go into my bobble head routine he reached over and turned on the recorder. Then he gave his mechanical recital of the Miranda Rights without even bothering to watch my head go up and down.

"You understand your rights, Leo? And that you waive those rights, and the information you are about to give is completely voluntary?"

Hearing him speak the words I'd only heard in movies and TV cop shows had made the cinnamon creep back into my mouth.

After a moment or two without hearing anything from me he

asked, "Would you like a glass of water, Leo?" His keen observation of my choking crow impersonation made him call out, "Mark, would you bring Mister Walker a glass of water?"

A minute or so later one of the investigators came out of my bathroom with a glass of water, set it on the coffee table in front of me, then went back to whatever it was he had been snooping into. I took a swallow, then emptied the glass.

"Want another?" Friday asked.

"No, thanks."

"Okay then. Why don't you start from when you first got the idea of getting a corpse from the morgue to where we are now. Just relax and speak in a normal voice."

I succumbed to his hypnotic suggestion, leaned back, stared at the ceiling, and recounted the tale of how Charlie's latest fiasco had unraveled my life. I decided to tell him everything. Even about the whiskey sour spilled in my lap.

When I had finished, Officer Friday sat for several moments without moving or saying a word. I finally had to break the suspense. "You don't believe me, do you?"

He cleared his throat, leaned forward and turned off the recorder, then shook his head. "Nobody could make up a story like that, Leo."

"So, are they going to send me to the Big House?"

"Where?"

"You know, the slammer, up the river, the joint."

"You mean *prison*, Leo?"

"That's where they usually send us criminals, isn't it?"

Friday smiled and patted my knee as he got off the couch. "I don't think you need to worry about that."

I felt more stunned than relieved. Then the stun gradually began to feel more like a soothing warm spa. Friday and all the cops in the world were back on my side. Or I was back on theirs.

He called out to the kitchen for Partner to bring Charlie back in. "And don't worry about Charlie," he said as he took out his cell phone and walked toward the kitchen. "He won't be going to the *Big House*, either."

Charlie was the least of my worries. I knew he wouldn't be going anywhere bad. If he ever did, the residents of the place would probably crown him king within a week. Then assign me as his jester.

Friday and Partner had a brief conversation before Friday went into the kitchen and Charlie returned to the couch next to me. Instead of Partner taking his usual perch on the arm of the couch, he sat in the big chair opposite us. That convinced me the worst of things had passed. I felt I could almost give him a hug now we were no longer adversaries. Or maybe a pat on the shoulder. Perhaps offer a handshake. I settled for a tiny smile in his direction. But that quickly melted away under his stony glare.

Charlie immediately filled me in on all the events that transpired while he was in the kitchen, which consisted mainly of the list of groceries he consumed. And the fact we now needed another delivery if I wanted anything to eat.

My stomach grumbled for attention, but I decided to wait and ask Friday for permission to call. Officer Partner might not be an adversary anymore, but he was still intimidating.

It wasn't long before Friday came back and sat on the couch next to me. He leaned back and looked at me. "All we have to do now is wait for the investigators to finish."

"Just exactly what," I asked, "do they have to finish?"

"They investigate crime scenes."

"But," the word *crime* instantly challenged my relieved feeling. "But you said I wasn't being accused of anything."

"And I meant it. But a crime *has* been committed in all this. More than likely, several crimes. The crime lab boys will help clear up some of the confusion."

"But in my house?"

"What they find, Leo, can clear you of things. Not necessarily point any fingers at you."

"What kind of fingers might find it necessary to point at me?"

His cell phone rang before he could answer. After a couple of "uh-uh's," and "I see's," he put the phone back in his pocket, got off the couch, and motioned Partner to join him in another private confab on the other side of the room.

I tried to hear what they were saying, but Charlie kept asking me if I thought they would let him call for some more groceries.

The crime lab crew finally tired of whatever it was they had been doing and filed out through the living room. They didn't join Friday and Partner in their confab, but one of them on the way out said over her shoulder, "We're done, Sergeant."

Detective Friday gave a short wave and returned to the couch. Officer Partner followed the investigators outside.

"Well, Leo, I think we're about done here."

"You mean it's all over?"

Charlie didn't wait for an answer. "Can I call for some food now?"

"Sure, Charlie," Friday said. "Go right ahead."

"That sounds to me like it's all over."

"Not quite Leo. But it's pretty much over for my partner and me. Fingerprints from Butch match some of those from several burglaries around town. The boys down at burglary think his sister is probably involved, too. Probably even one or more of the people in that car you saw."

"You mean they're all criminals?"

"Looks like it. It shouldn't be hard to track down the sister-you-don't-know and the others now. Not with your description of the car they're driving, and that traffic pile up. Burglary Division will handle them."

"Wow. What do you think will happen to her?"

Friday shrugged. "Oh, she'll probably get about three or five."

"Three or five what?"

"Years. In the *Big House*."

I thought about that for a minute. "Do you think she might be mad at me for giving you a description of the car and come after me when she gets out?"

"I wouldn't worry about it."

"Of course not. You carry a badge and a gun."

"No, Leo. Those people are burglars. Not killers."

"I don't have to testify against them in court, do I?"

"Of course not. They probably will never even know about you."

"She saw me with her brother."

"You're making too much of this, Leo. Let's get back to your present situation. You and Charlie still have a little more to do."

I had a pretty good idea what the word *little* involved when Charlie said it. Coming from a policeman, I fully expected a nine-point-six on the Richter Scale. All I could manage was a weak, "What do we have to do?"

"My partner is bringing in a couple of forms we'll fill out. You and Charlie will have to be charged with abuse of a corpse. Then you go in front of a judge."

"But, but, you said we weren't going to jail."

"You're not going to jail, Leo. Take a couple of deep breaths. These are only misdemeanor charges. Just plead guilty, tell the judge you're sorry, and that you won't ever do it again. A little slap on the wrist, and you'll be on your way."

There was that word *little* again.

It was two months before Charlie and I went to court. I had strongly declined hiring Charlie's lawyer friend in favor of one I saw advertised on the side of a city bus.

The trial didn't last long. Didn't even make the six o'clock news. The judge didn't look anything at all like a real judge. At least not what I imagined one to look like. This one was nothing like the wise grandfatherly type. Partly due, I'm sure, to the fact she was much too young.

Our lawyer assured us she would be lenient, though. Mainly because this was our first offense, and it was only a misdemeanor. The hardest part was convincing Charlie we really were guilty of corpse abuse. He insisted John got only the very best treatment from us. Up until he got thrown out of the van onto the street, that is. But Charlie contended that was purely accidental. I finally had to bribe him with a trip to an all-you-can-eat restaurant before he would plead guilty.

We each received six months' probation, and twenty hours of community service. Charlie got his twenty hours on the night shift at the county morgue. I was assigned trash pick-up in the part of the city that included Sycamore Street.

Some things worked out fairly well, though. All things considered. I still have my job after the end of my disastrous vacation. On the other hand, my credit card is maxed out, and the grocery store bill is still racking up interest. There's a long list of accident victims from the one-way street carnage hounding me for vehicle damages and minor medical bills. The used car lot is threatening to repo the van if I don't make a payment soon. And the city code enforcement officer will soon be coming around again to check on where the van is parked. But it needs some gas before I can drive it to the front of the house where it will be ticketed as an abandoned vehicle because I can't afford new plates.

Charlie's mother called the other day to say hello, and to tell me he has a foolproof plan to get me out of what she called my "little problems."

Of course, that still leaves the question of how forgiving Melissa will be over the treatment of her brother's corpse when she gets out of the *Big House.*

And then the drunk blond on Sycamore Street might spot me while I'm picking up empty beer cans and broken bottles down by *The Starlight Lounge.* But there's a chance she won't remember me. Or realize I didn't have anything to do with the death of her future husband. Or that somebody finally convinced her John wasn't really Mike. Or she may have sobered up. All those things could be possible.

If I was Charlie.

End

POSITIVE THOUGHTS

Here are a few words of encouragement to help you when things in your life unexpectedly go freakish. It might be something as minor as breaking the point off your pencil, to waking up on Judgment Day the morning after you screamed at the heavens, "I don't need no stinkin' god."

Bad things have no doubt been happening to you for a long time now. And you probably nod and smile at bumper stickers like, *shit happens*, or *life's a bitch and then you die*. Even deep down you're probably smiling. That's because you're eyeball deep in denial. You can't even smell your coffee in the morning without getting a snootfull of that crocodile infested river.

You may have been blaming all your ills on an overbearing mother, bullies, or some inadequate body part. If so, you have been rowing up the wrong creek. None of those things are to blame for your chaotic life. The truth you have been ignoring all these years is that Life is out to get you, and there's not a damn thing you can do about it. You are too weak and puny. Life is not only a bitch, she's a big, *strong* bitch.

But here are some helpful suggestions on how to live with things the way they are. Unfortunately, they will not aid you in dealing with an overbearing mother, overcoming bullies, or compensating for any inadequate body parts. You're on your own there.

Once you have cowed down to the Big Bitch Of Life, and admitted to yourself you have no alternative but to accept all the horrible things she has planned to throw at you, it is time to slink into a corner of your pitiful mind and deal with things the best you can. Your chances of success in coping from here on, though, will probably be no better than before. Still, you might take some consolation in knowing everything is completely beyond your control. You may even manage a weak grin from time to time.

See? You're beginning to feel better already.

The thing you need to do with this revelation now is to panic. It's okay. Go ahead and get it over with. Things are going to get a lot worse as time drags by. You will need all the wits you can muster when the next King-Kong-sized monkey wrench jars you out of the delusion you might ever grasp even a sliver of a normal life.

As your panic mode winds down, you will notice the bad things happening to you are probably getting worse. But maybe at a slower rate. If so, take full advantage of it. This would be the time to count your blessings. There will be very few opportunities to do so after this brief lull as more disastrous and catastrophic events will appear around every corner in your pathetic life. You are now at what is often called the *point of diminishing returns*. In other words, no matter what you do from now on, things are only going to get worse by the minute.

There will, however, be brief rays of sunshine in your wretched existence once in a while. For instance, even though your own life is pointless, there will be no end of good news about your relatives and friends you can celebrate. For instance, there will be things like your ex remarrying an award winning author and winning the lottery.

Perhaps your coworkers netted ten thousand bucks each on a stock tip, but you disregarded that tip for a different one and lost two grand. Maybe each of your friends in the neighborhood lost twenty pounds in your shared diet, while you gained eight. Or, your only son and a hooker fell in love and agreed to have sex-change operations, and marry each other in a tribal ceremony in the Amazon jungle. Live. On 60 Minutes.

Be happy for all of them, and wish them well. Their good fortune is the closest you will ever come to having any of your own. Always keep in mind you have absolutely no control over the misery in your life. Learn to accept it gracefully. At least in public.

Feel free to refer back to these few positive words as you slog your way through one catastrophe after another throughout your worthless life. Perhaps they will give you the strength and fortitude to forge ahead.

But I doubt it.

End

PIECE OF CAKE

Thanks to my Aunt Emma my sweet tooth has gone sour, and I'm now out of trash bags.

To be fair, it wasn't all her fault. Granted, she is not the most charming person on the planet. She never married, but it wasn't because she hated men. And it wasn't because she was the old maid stereotype who wasted away her youth pining over some real or imaginary lost love. It was just that men couldn't stand to be around her.

Now I'm not the jealous type, but I got tired of her superior smile when everyone would ooh and ah over the cakes she brought to family functions. It wasn't as if she had a special talent no one else had. What she did have was a cookbook from somebody's great-great whoever with all those scrumptious recipes.

Still, I wouldn't mind if the folks gushed over me for a change. Instead of oohs and ahs at those gatherings, all I ever get are questions about why I'm not already married with a houseful of kids. What's so wrong about just being happy instead?

What I needed was one of those recipes. That way I could simply toss a cake together and take it to the next family shindig. Then when everyone tasted what a great job a lowly bachelor like me could do, those oohs and ahs would be heaped on me. Of course, I wouldn't want Aunt Emma to know how I beat her at her own game. It would be a challenge, but I felt up to it.

With a loosely formed plan I boldly dialed her number. It rang about eleven times before she picked up her phone and demanded, "What do you want?"

"Hi, Aunt Emma. This is your nephew, James."

"I don't know any James."

"Jimmy." I hadn't gone by that name since grade school. "Edith's boy."

"Oh. What do you want?"

"How have you been, Aunt Emma?"

"Fine. What do you want?"

"Do you still happen to have that old family recipe book?"

"Of course I do."

"I, uh, wanted to copy a recipe out of it."

"Well, why didn't you say so right off?"

I hadn't expected challenges this soon, but I rose to the occasion. "I was just making small talk."

"Well stop it."

"Yes, Ma'am. May I copy a recipe from your recipe book?"

"Which one?"

The reasons for her marital status was becoming more clear to me. "For a pie."

"Fine. When?"

"How about in an hour or two?"

"Well, which is it?"

"An hour."

"Fine."

With that final "fine," she simply hung up and went about

whatever it was she did when she wasn't making somebody sweat over the phone. Maybe constructing a gingerbread house in the backyard, and firing up her oven.

I grabbed a pen, small notebook, and drove across town. I pulled into her driveway and waited until an exact hour had passed. Then I remembered how dear aunty felt about "newfangled gadgets," so I left my cellphone on the seat under an almost empty Zippy's Hamburgers sack. Didn't want *The William Tell Overture* blasting out in case somebody called me while I was inside.

After ringing the doorbell and knocking a dozen or so times, Aunt Emma opened the door. It had been a year since I'd seen her, but she hadn't changed. Her grey hair was still worn in a tight bun, she still wore those clunky shoes with the short heels, and she still wore a long faded cotton dress. And her smile was still safely tucked away in a drawer somewhere.

"What do you want?"

"I came for the recipe, Aunt Emma."

"Then you must be Jimmy. Wipe your feet and come in."

I dutifully wiped my feet on the spotless door mat with an embroidered goose wearing a bonnet above the word WELCOME.

When we entered her cozy kitchen, she took the old recipe book from the counter and laid it on the table. It was huge.

Her small round table sat in the middle of the kitchen, and I took the first chair as I entered. She took the chair to my right and opened the book. "Now, what kind of pie did you want to bake?"

"Well, I thought maybe I could kinda look through the pie section and pick out one that sounded good."

"Ain't no such a thing as a pie section. Recipes were just put in here whenever a body had a mind to save one. You get to where you kind of remember where certain things are. Now what kind of pie do you want to bake?"

The old gal was as good at throwing out challenges as she was as throwing out suitors. Now I not only had to copy a cake recipe without her seeing me do it, I also had to find one. "Uh, well. . ."

She got up and walked to the sink. "You think on it while I make us some tea."

I pulled the book in front of me and casually turned a few pages. The first page had a recipe for bread pudding alongside detailed steps for rendering a hog. Another page gave tips on how to prevent wrinkles with bacon grease and vinegar, pickling watermelon rinds, a cure for hiccups, and a biscuit recipe at the bottom. There had to be over two hundred pages of recipes, assorted tips, and advice pasted willy-nilly throughout the thing.

Aunt Emma set two cups of tea on the table and sat down next to me. "Guess you see what I meant about finding a particular recipe now."

"Yes, Ma'am." Then inspiration struck. "Aunt Emma, would you do me a big favor and bake a batch of your famous cookies?"

Her face lit up, and I knew I'd found her weak spot. "You mean my pecan and chocolate chip cookies?"

"If it wouldn't be too much trouble."

"I didn't think you liked my baked goods the way you act at family doings. Come dessert time, you always look as if you're being forced to eat a piece of my cake."

"That's just because I like your cookies so much better."

She cracked open the drawer where she kept her smile. Not much, but enough to give a hint it was still in there.

"I suppose I could. But I can't very well bake cookies and find a pie recipe for you at the same time."

"Oh, that's okay. I'll just look through the book at all the neat things in here while you're making the cookies."

She got up and began to assemble pots and pans and the ingredients for the cookies, while I flipped through the pages. I needed to find a cake recipe, but I also needed to find one for a pie to copy down for her benefit.

She had already started mixing the cookie batter by the time I ran across a pie. She was more organized than I had counted on. Time was getting tight. I kept one finger on the pie page and continued my cake search. I flipped the pages faster and faster past things like how to pluck a turkey, when to plant rutabagas, where to build your outhouse, how to console a crying baby with laudanum, making carrot stew, pan-fried rattlesnake, setting a broken bone, and brewing beer.

It took me almost halfway through the book before I happened across a cake.

"Would you like another cup of tea, Jimmy?"

I flipped the pages back to the pie recipe, but kept my thumb on the cake page. "Uh, do you have to make some more?"

"Yes, but it doesn't take long."

"In that case, yes. Please."

When she turned to the sink to make the tea, I quickly flipped to the cake recipe and began to scribble it down in my notebook. It was tricky business. I had to keep my finger on the pie page so I could flip back to it when she turned around, which meant I couldn't hold my notebook still while I wrote in it. My phone could have solved the problem with a quick picture of the recipes, but I figured this was probably the last of the major challenges, so I pushed on.

I had copied only a few items before she came over to the table and picked up my cup and returned to the counter. I barely had enough time to flip the cake page to the pie again. Then, I had to turn to a blank page in my notebook and copy some of the pie ingredients before she came back and set the fresh tea on the table.

"Oh," she said as she looked at the open book, "I see you found a pie. But where are you going to find fresh rhubarb this time of year?"

"Rhubarb? Why would I want rhubarb?"

"Because that's the kind of pie recipe you're copying."

"It is? I mean, yes, it is. I've always wanted to make one. Of course, I won't start on it till rhubarb season gets here. Then I'll go out and get one. Maybe get a couple. Save one for later on."

She gave me a look to let me know her smile drawer had slammed shut. Fortunately, her cookie making duties were more important than giving me one of her scathing opinions. I resumed my scribbling as soon as she turned back to her cookie cooking things.

It was tricky business flipping back and forth with the pages every time Aunt Emma turned around to see if I might be doing something she could disapprove of, but after nearly half an hour I figured I had all the important cake stuff copied. The pie recipe was even in my notebook.

Yet one more challenge had to be dealt with before I could claim victory with my recipe venture. I wasn't sure how much longer it would take her to finish those famous cookies, but I didn't want to sit around and wait for them.

While I tried to think of a quick exit scheme a movement on the wall caught my attention. It was a plastic black and white cat. It continuously swung its tail in one direction while its eyes flicked in the opposite direction. Like clockwork. In fact, it was a clock. Sweet inspiration.

"Aunt Emma," I said in my most apologetic voice, "I just remembered I have an appointment across town in a few minutes."

"You can't wait for thirty minutes? Cookies will be about done by then."

"Gee, I'd really like to, but I gave my word I'd be there."

"Well, in that case, you'd better go. Will you be back today?"

I grabbed my notebook as I got up. "Probably be tomorrow before I can come back for the cookies."

"Make sure you call first. I don't like surprises."

"Of course," I said as I headed out the door. "Thanks for the recipes, I mean the pie recipe."

I backed out of her drive and drove to a supermarket I noticed on the way there. It probably had some of the things I needed for the cake.

About a mile away I came to the Farmer Boy's Megamart. It certainly looked big enough. I out-maneuvered a guy in a polished sports car for a parking spot close to the front door. It pays to already have a few dings in your car when challenging somebody for a parking space.

I went inside and immediately understood the *mega* part. An ant wandering into a football stadium during the Super Bowl probably has the same sensation. Even the grocery carts were huge. The size of everything and the packed crowd were so overwhelming I was tempted to turn around and look for a less *mega* supermart.

Before I could take another step, though, a young man dressed in red bib overalls and a red and white checkered shirt blocked my way with a megacart. "Welcome to Farmer Boy's Megamart, sir. Is this your first shopping experience here, or do you already have a Farmer Boy's discount shoppers' card?"

I read the name tag on his shirt, FARMER TED AT YOUR SERVICE. He also wore a bright yellow plastic hat designed to look like it was made of straw. "Uh, no. This is my first time."

"Well, welcome, sir."

"You already said that."

"Yes, but we here at Farmer Boy's never get tired of saying it. Welcome! And to make your shopping more enjoyable, you can use the computer here on your megacart to enter your pertinent information."

He turned on the computer and the screen lit up with blazing red letters, WELCOME SHOPPER. He punched a key and the screen showed, ENTER NAME. "By entering the information it asks for, sir you will be entitled to mega discounts throughout the store."

"What kind of information?"

"Oh, just the usual kind of things companies ask for."

"Like what?"

"You know, date of birth, social security number, sleeping habits, next of kin. Those sort of things. You can type it all in while you shop. Then your discount card will be waiting for you at the checkout register."

"How important is it to have one of those cards?"

He looked around, then whispered in my ear, "I'm not supposed to say anything," he glanced around again, "but you can save a bundle with one."

Well that settled it. I was not about to pass up saving a bundle on something. "Can you tell me where the cake stuff is?"

He pointed to my right as he grabbed an empty megacart and

rushed to another customer who just came in. "Check the information board over there. And enjoy your shopping experience."

What he had pointed to was a sign the size of monster billboard. A giant red arrow hung from the distant ceiling and pointed straight down in front of it. I gave my megacart a hearty shove in that direction and began to type in my pertinent information as I walked. While trying to remember things like my maternal grandmother's maiden name and her birthday, I accidently bumped into a megacart pushed by an attractive woman in shorts and wearing a T-shirt with WWJD printed across the front.

It was only a slight tap, and the megacarts appeared to be constructed out of steel girders. They could probably withstand a high-speed collision with an eighteen wheeler and come out ahead. But you couldn't tell that from her reaction.

Her looks instantly went from serene to an attacking Marine. She screamed out above the din of shoppers, "What the hell's wrong with you? Don't you have any concept at all about shopping etiquette?"

I had no idea what that was. But before she screamed out enough information for me to figure it out, a bubbly young lady dressed like Farmer Ted suddenly appeared. Her name tag proclaimed she was FARMERETTE CINDY. She pranced over and whooped, "Welcome shoppers! I have coupons for you both."

The offended lady's screams stopped as if someone had flipped a switch, and her menacing looks were replaced by a broad smile. She snatched all the coupons with one deft move, gave me one last scowl, and joined the throng of other shoppers. I couldn't be sure, but it looked like she banged into a couple of megacarts that got in her way. There weren't any outbursts about shopping etiquette, though, so maybe I was mistaken.

Farmerette Cindy noticed my bewildered look and asked, "Is there anything I can help you with, sir?"

"Well, as a matter of fact there is. I need some cake making stuff."

"This your first time here at Farmer Boy's?"

"Very first."

"Then follow me and I'll introduce you to our information board."

In no time at all we reached the big board and stood on the exact spot where the huge arrow pointed. YOU ARE HERE was printed on the board near the bottom next to a red X. I was fairly sure I understood that, but Farmerette Cindy explained it to me anyway.

"See this big X here?" She pointed to it while looking at me to make certain I saw it. When she saw me nod and was convinced I saw the X, she continued. "Well, this is where we are in relation to the rest of the store." She paused a moment to make sure I got that, too. "The rest of the information board is just a big map showing all the departments. See?"

"Uh, huh."

She wasn't convinced. "Let me show you. Over here," and she motioned for me to follow to the left side of the board, "is an index with all the major categories in the store. "Let's say you want to buy, oh, a saddle for instance. We look up the word saddle in the index," she looked up saddle and pointed it out to me, "and we see the index shows they are located on aisle 147 of the Equestrian Section in the Northeastern Quadrant. See?"

"Uh, huh. But I don't want to ride a horse. I want to make a cake."

"Then I suggest you begin with the baking section." She turned back to the index, then gave me directions to that quadrant. "And should you ever need help locating anything while enjoying your shopping experience, there are always Farmer Boy farmers and farmerettes patrolling the aisles to assist you."

I smiled to show my appreciation and said, "That's nice to know. Big as this place is it'd be easy to get lost."

She smiled back to show me she could and said, "We used to tell customers to drop breadcrumbs behind them as they shopped so they could find their way back. But our efficient workers always swept up the crumbs as soon as they hit the floor. So now we have an army of friendly farmers and farmerettes to keep folks from getting lost."

She looked at me for several moments until she realized I wasn't going to react. "It's just a little store joke."

"Uh, huh. Well, I'm going to the baking section now. Thanks for your help."

"You're welcome. And welcome to Farmer Boy's. Enjoy your shopping experience!"

I headed off in the direction she had pointed, being careful not to violate any shopping etiquette along the way. It was tricky business with the press of shoppers going every which-way, and me not knowing the etiquette thing. Except for the not hitting somebody's megacart part, of course.

Entering the pertinent information was getting harder to deal with, too. When it asked if I had pets I accidently hit the YES key. Then it asked what kind. I don't have any pets, but there was no way to go back and change it. So, I went along with it and pushed the key to indicate a dog. It immediately asked for its name, breed, age, and its veterinarian's name. Then it was a choice of numerous brands of dog food I fed it and where I normally bought it.

During all that I almost violated shopping etiquette several times. In the last close encounter, I managed to avoid cart contact by veering away at the last minute and ramming a couple of stacked displays instead. There was an incredible din with hundreds of clattering cans up and down the aisle, but at least nobody screamed at me.

After things quieted down, I took a break from entering pertinent information and looked at some of the merchandise on the shelves. There were all kinds of foods and other things on sale. I grabbed some donuts, couple bags of chips, a jar of pickled herring, and just couldn't resist some gizmo reduced fifty-percent and had something to do with pineapples.

It seemed I should've reached the baking section by this time, so I looked around for a farmer or farmerette for directions. They should've been easy to spot with their bright red and yellow clothes. Plus the plastic hat. Even when I unfolded the megacart's handy ladder and climbed up several steps, I still couldn't spot one.

Although I did spot a cart that wasn't zipping up and down the aisles like most of the others. I climbed down, folded the ladder back in place, and made my way to the stationary cart. It was manned by an older, well dressed gentleman, who sat on the cart's foldout recliner reading a book. I put on my best smile. "Excuse me, sir. Have you seen one of the farmers or farmerettes around here?"

He lowered his book and smiled back. "You're new to these parts, aren't you?"

"As a matter of fact, I'm new to all the parts from the front door. That's why I'm trying to find one of those farmer people."

His smile got bigger. "Well, son, that's not likely to happen."

"But they told me up front they were all over the place."

"Maybe, maybe not." He took his glasses off and carefully wiped them off with his handkerchief. "Truth is, not many folks ever seen one. Not up close, anyhow. Some say they scurry around atop the shelves where nobody can see 'em. Others say they don't exist at all."

"What do you think, sir?"

"Don't make no difference to me one way or the other." He sighed and put his glasses back on. "My wife likes to come here and leave me with the cart while she shops around. I used to move the cart to another aisle after she'd go off and hope she wouldn't find me. She always did. Now, I just stay where she leaves me and daydream about her gettin' lost in here and never coming back. Either way, I probably have about much chance of seeing one of those farmer fellas as she has of gettin' lost."

"That's sad."

"What's sad, you not finding one of those farmer fellas, or my marital train wreck?"

"Both, I guess."

He looked at me through tired eyes. "Yeah, you're right. Both for sure. Tell you what. You seem to be a decent sort." He motioned me closer and continued in a low voice. "Let me give you a tip. Listen to the PA system. Whenever it says something about a clean-up on some aisle, get on over there and you might catch one. But you gotta be quick. Don't take 'em but a blink of an eye to clean something up and leave nothin' behind but a wet floor sign."

With all the other things going on around me, I hadn't paid any attention the PA system. "Thanks a lot, sir. I'll listen for that." I wasn't sure if it would be proper to wish him luck on losing his wife. To play it safe as I moved on I just said, "I hope you enjoy your shopping experience."

I set off again in the general direction I had first started. Only now, the PA system also competed for my attention along with entering pertinent information, looking for the baking section, and trying to avoid any shopping etiquette mistakes.

The PA soon won out with the announcement, ATTENTION SHOPPERS. TO MAKE YOUR SHOPPING EXPERIENCE MORE ENJOYABLE, FEEL FREE TO TAKE ADVANTAGE OF THE NUMEROUS SOFT DRINK MACHINES LOCATED THROUGHOUT THE STORE, FILLED WITH REASONABLY PRICED ICE COLD BEVERAGES.

Before the ringing in my ears stopped from the announcement, I managed to avoid a shopping etiquette blunder by yanking the emergency brake on my megacart. It came to an immediate halt. I halted a split second later when my cart's airbag deployed.

The other cart's operator looked so old and frail, she probably forgot how many years ago she celebrated her 100th birthday. "Are you okay, young man?" she asked.

I gingerly felt my nose. Fortunately, the airbag hadn't broken it, and it didn't bleed much. "I'm fine. You weren't frightened, were you?"

"Gracious no. Everybody in here usually just rams into you instead of trying to stop."

"Oh. Well, this is my first time here. Have you seen the baking section anywhere?"

"No, this is my first time here, too. And I don't do much cooking these days."

"I understand. There comes a time to slow down in life."

"That's for sure. About the only thing I spend time doing now is just breaking wild horses. By the way, have you seen any saddles?"

"Uh, no. But I think they're over on aisle 147 in the Equestrian Section of the Northeastern Quadrant."

"Why thank you very much, sonny. And I hope you find your baking things." She patted my hand and scraped her cart along the side of mine on her way to the buckaroo area.

I gave my cart a hearty push and continued my quest up and down the aisles. As I turned a corner to explore in another direction, I inadvertently knocked a jug of olives off the shelf. It shattered and sent a wall of stuffed olives down the aisle pushed by a river of olive juice. I started to make my getaway from the crime scene when the PA blared, CLEAN UP ON AISLE SIXTY-SEVEN. I then remembered what the old man had said about catching one of the farmer folk at a cleanup. But by the time I brought my megacart to a stop and got it turned around, all I saw was a damp spot on the floor with a plastic WET FLOOR cone on top. I thought I heard some scrabbling sounds at the top of the shelves, but wasn't sure.

It was back to whatever numbered square I seemed to be stuck on. Just before I succumbed to total despair, however, I rounded a corner and found myself at the baking section. It was a dazzling array of brilliant aluminum and stainless steel pots, pans, bowls, spoons, spatulas, and strange shiny things. I grabbed everything I saw with the word cake on its label. Then I picked up some bowls, spoons, and even some things without a label—just in case they might have something to do with a cake. I was beginning to appreciate the mega part of my cart.

The dairy section was next on my list, but it was much easier to find. I saw the twenty-foot high black and white cow from less than a quarter mile away. I could even make out the four, three-foot-long balloons hanging from its belly near the rear. I never did understand why a cow is always around dairy stuff.

The milk section was in keeping with the Farmer Boy's Megamarket image. I was amazed by the vast selections. Milk was in my notebook, but I wasn't sure if it was for the cake or the pie. There was no mention of a specific kind in either recipe, though. I was sure of that. So I simply picked up a large container with the biggest letters of milk on its label.

Farther into the dairy section brought me to the eggs. Like the milk, they didn't come in one kind either. Or in one size. Not even the same color. The more I looked the more confused I got. I finally grabbed, gently, one dozen medium eggs without looking at what color they were. I was pretty sure I'd only need the inside of them anyway.

Before I entered the butter section I stopped at one of the soft drink machines with the reasonably priced beverages. All the walking, and major decisions I had been making, had given me a healthy thirst. Unfortunately, the machine kept flashing a red digital notice exact change was required, and I didn't have a ten-dollar bill, ten ones, or a five and five ones.

The butter section turned out to be worse than either the milk or the egg section. It not only had butter, it had spreads of every conceivable kind to spread on anything you could think of. In a fit of exasperation, I grabbed a six-pound tub of Megamart spread. I didn't see how I could possibly go wrong with it. It promised to be even better than butter.

By now I was getting used to the size and endless selections of the place. So when I found the flour zone, I simply picked up two ten-pound sacks and resisted the urge to read past the word FLOUR on the labels.

Sugar proved to be the easiest item on my list. I saw a sack of sugar in an unattended megacart and helped myself. I rounded the nearest corner mere seconds ahead of a shrill scream behind me. "All right, you low life scum-sucking low life that took my sugar! Don't you know the meaning of shopping etiquette?"

Her voice sounded kind of familiar, but I didn't hang around to see who screamed it.

The loaded megacart was getting harder to push with everything in it by this time. And I was pretty sure I had all the cake stuff I needed, so I fell in behind a line of carts all moving toward what I hoped was the checkout area.

My hope was rewarded after a few hundred yards when the checkout registers came into view. I quickly analyzed the different lines at the dozens of registers and spotted one that looked to be the shortest. I split from the line I was in and violated shopping etiquette just enough to beat out two other shoppers with the same destination in mind.

My reward for finishing first came a minute later in the register line of my choice when the checkout girl said into her microphone, "Price check on a sixteen ounce can of Farmer Boy's rhubarb at register thirty-eight." She then calmly began to file her nails.

I heard groans ahead of me and behind me. None of them as loud as mine.

It was too late to move to another line. A large woman and three unruly children had me penned in from behind with a megacart loaded down with even more stuff in it than mine. She alternated between glaring at the oblivious checkout girl, and shrieking terrifying threats at her energetic offspring.

While I waited, and the checkout girl continued to grind away her nails, the woman's threatening shrieks were temporarily drowned out by a PA announcement, MEGACART TOWING NEEDED ON AISLE 147 IN THE EQUESTRIAN SECTION.

The mystery of the rhubarb price was finally resolved and I moved into the action position next to the whizzing conveyor belt. After a twenty-minute wait while my Farmer Boy's discount card was activated, I barely had time to place my things on the belt before the girl rang them up. The lights on the register flashed with an alarming speed, and increasing totals.

On the other side of the register a hyper teenager, dancing to the sounds from somewhere inside his head, shoved everything into plastic bags and tossed them into an empty megacart next to him.

The barely awake checkout girl wiped a wisp of hair from her forehead and informed me of the purchase total flashing in front of me. I acted as if I wasn't at all surprised at the astronomical sum, and nonchalantly inserted my credit card. All the while offering up a silent prayer it wouldn't be declined.

She gathered up my register receipt and piled it on top of the waiting megacart. I declined the sacker's offer to help me to my car. The only tip I could afford after this purchase was, "Just say no to drugs." I don't think he heard me.

When I got back to my apartment I unloaded all the sacks from the back seat and set them on the kitchen counter, on top of the fridge, and on the floor. Then I unloaded the sacks in the trunk.

After everything was inside, I piled as many of the pots, pans, and utensils as possible on the table. But I made sure there was still a little room left for me to create my cake masterpiece. There wasn't enough room for the pineapple thingy anywhere, so it went in the fridge.

I arranged my four chairs close to the table where I would be standing and stacked most of the ingredients on them. It was a little like a conductor must feel when he steps in front of his orchestra. But it was now time to become a gourmet baker. I placed my notebook on the table where it would be easy to read. I quickly discovered my first challenge was to decipher my hurried scribbles.

The next challenge was to decide whether or not I had mixed some of the pie recipe in with the one for the cake. Then I had to figure out the correct order of steps. I bravely tackled the first one.

The cake called for heating the cook stove, and getting it too hot to hold your hand at the back of the oven while saying *mulberry bushes* three times.

Of course I don't have an old fashioned cook stove, but I do have an electric stove with an oven. I figured it should work just as good. The control dial for the oven has numbers from 0 to 550. It doesn't say what they mean, so I set it halfway at 275. There was also the question of whether or not to leave the oven door open. I decided to shut it in case I had to walk past it, since my kitchen is pretty small. I'd do the mulberry bushes thing later when the cake was ready to cook.

The next step was much simpler. All it called for was to separate two eggs.

I took the egg carton from a nearby chair and opened it to make sure it still held two good eggs. After the gyrations of the sacker kid, all bets were off on anything fragile surviving his sacker style. But all twelve of them looked okay. From the outside anyway. Unfortunately, the other *okay* things around me began to go the other way about that time.

Holding the open carton in my left hand, I leaned forward over the table and reached for a stack of small bowls. My forward lean proved to be a mistake. Every one of the eggs tumbled out onto the middle of the table. All but one broke.

Eleven broken eggs mixed in with their shells was bad enough, but I also discovered my table was not level. As I picked out the biggest pieces of egg shells the broken eggs slowly flowed away from me toward the other side of the table.

As bad as things looked, I managed to remain calm. I quickly glanced at my notebook and noticed the word yolks on the page. With *separate two eggs,* and then *yolks* on the page, it stood to reason two yolks would also be needed later on.

I tossed the empty carton to the floor and grabbed a measuring cup and a big spoon. The yolks were all broken and mingled among the whites, but I managed to dip out what looked like two yolks into the measuring cup. I set the cup on the closest chair and gently set the remaining unbroken egg next to it. It had grit. Like me.

Then I turned to the task of separating two eggs from the mess. I leaned on the table and reached for the stack of small bowls again. When I did the table tilted back toward me, and the eggs stopped their steady flow to the other side. I did a few experiments and found if I leaned on the table a little it remained level. That gave me enough time to spoon out more or less the equivalent of one complete egg into each of two bowls. Hardly any egg shells mixed in with them.

While I transferred the bowls of eggs to the kitchen counter, I had an idea how to clean up the mess on the table. Since the blob flowed to one side, all I had to do was hold a bowl under the table edge on that side and let it flow into the bowl.

I picked up a bowl that looked big enough and moved everything else out of the way, and held it under the table edge. After holding it for a minute or so, I got tired of the slow progress of the egg flow and tried something else.

I walked back around the table and bent my legs enough to catch my belt buckle under the edge. As I stood a little straighter, the table lifted on my side and the eggs flowed faster to the other side. All I needed now was to reach across the table with the bowl and catch the eggs as they poured over the edge.

Unfortunately, as I stood up all the way in order to get the bowl in place on the other side, the table also moved up with me. That sent the egg pool into a torrent of raw omelet into and around the bowl. Mostly around it. It also sent everything else on the table crashing to the floor and into the mess of eggs that missed the bowl. My open notebook was the last thing to land on top of the gooey eggs.

My calm state of mind had been reduced to a *somewhat* calm, but I still remained confident.

As I stood at the sink wiping off my notebook, I decided the first step had gone relatively well, all things considered. I had more-or-less two egg yolks in a cup, and more-or-less two separated eggs. Also, there was a big bowl with some eggs in that. Hardly any egg shells in any of it.

Three more deep breaths and I was ready to tackle step two. According to the blurred writing in my notebook, thanks to the egg goo, I now needed to measure and sift three cups of flour. I picked up one of the two ten-pound flour bags and set it on the table. The sifting part threw me at first, but since the bag bragged about being self-rising, I figured it was probably self sifting as well.

The first thing I found out about flour was it didn't open as easy as a bag of chips. As it turned out there were other things to learn about it, too. But that was the first one.

After trying to rip open the bag with my bare hands and getting nowhere fast, I grabbed a butcher knife and sawed the top off. Now I had easy access to the contents, as well as a dusting of flour on the table, me, and the egg goo that hadn't made it to the floor. Maybe a little more like a *healthy* dusting.

Next, I needed a measuring cup. It still sat on the chair where I had put it. Holding two yolks.

My somewhat calm state of mind downgraded into more of a *fragile* calm.

I dumped the yolks into a small pan with a handle on it and rinsed out the cup. Then I found a bowl big enough to hold three cups of flour. I dipped the cup into the open bag but it didn't get quite full, so I set it on the table and poured some more into it from the bag. It got the cup full. With a generous overflow onto the table.

After leveling off the cup with my finger, I emptied it into the bowl. More precisely, I emptied all the flour that didn't stick to the inside of the wet cup. I washed the cup and made sure it was dry this time.

Now because some of the flour had stuck to the cup, the bowl actually held a little less than a full cup, so I poured it all back into the bag. All that didn't spill onto the table and the floor, of course.

Once again I poured some flour into the cup and discovered another interesting fact about flour. It does not pour out of a bag in a predictable manner. What may start as a slow trickle will suddenly dump a bucketful of the dusty stuff over everything. The flour buildup was getting pretty deep on the table, so I set the measuring cup down and pushed the excess into a pile away from my work area. I figured the flour would soak up the egg spillage and make it all easier to clean up after I finished cooking the cake.

As I was about to pick up the measuring cup again, I noticed the flour must've settled a little. I poured some more into it and tapped it on the table several times to make sure it held exactly one full cup.

Luckily, I bought two bags of flour. With all the tamping, pouring, and spilling there wasn't much left in the first one. I opened the second bag with a little better luck. Not by much, but I welcome any improvement in my life, no matter how small.

When I finally got the third cup in the bowl, it became obvious it wouldn't hold much of anything else but the flour. I knew there were more ingredients, so I emptied it all into a large bowl.

After once more pushing excess flour aside, I checked my notebook through the lingering flour haze. The next step required a bit of deciphering. I had written *lg bol mix 1/4 c butt 2 c sug 2 c mil.* It obviously meant mix butter, sugar, and milk of those amounts in a large bowl. Crystal clear. Also crystal clear to me was the fact my only large bowl now contained three cups of flour.

The next largest bowl in my culinary collection looked as if it would hold the three cups of flour, but it now held about half a dozen raw scrambled eggs. With hardly any shells in them.

My fragile calm turned into mild exasperation.

I grabbed the next size bowl and poured the egg mess into it. Or at least all that didn't spill onto the table or floor.

Then I washed the large bowl and moved on to the butter part. Since I'd bought a spread instead of butter, I didn't know if a quarter cup of spread would still be a quarter of a cup when melted. I decided to scoop some out, melt it, then pour out just a quarter cup of it.

My search for a pan ended with the discovery that the only pan with a handle now held the two egg yolks.

Exasperation went up a huge notch.

I looked around for a bowl or anything to put the yolks in, but everything seemed to have something in it. And more than likely the *something* would be needed somewhere else down the line. Or at least I was sure it would be if I put the something anywhere other than where it was now.

My exasperation drooped closer to despair as I plopped onto a chair to think things out. Onto the chair with the remaining unbroken egg, which instantly ceased to be unbroken. The egg's grit, and mine, also ceased.

I sat in the midst of little self-made hell wondering about the purpose of my life. Before I could come up with anything positive my introspection was shattered by *The William Tell Overture*.

I found my cellphone under the megamart receipt pile and wrapped my egg and flour covered hand around it. I tried to give a cherry, "Hello."

"Jimmy?"

"Yes, Aunt Emma."

"Well, why didn't you say so right off instead of making me ask?"

"I'm sorry. It won't happen again."

"See that it doesn't. Did you keep your word?"

"Uh, about what?"

"About keeping your appointment. Are you getting daft, boy?"

"Oh, my appointment. Yes, Ma'am."

"Good. Then you can still come back for your cookies today. And stop at the store and get me something on your way over."

"I'd be happy to."

"What, happy to get the cookies, or happy to do something for me?"

"Well, both, really."

"Uh, huh. Well, just before you get to my house there's a big grocery store."

"I know."

"Fine. Pop in there and pick me up one of their fresh baked cakes."

"Reality and *The Twilight Zone* silently fought for control in my mind for several moments as I gazed out over my kitchen battlefield. Her voice brought me back to whichever world I occupied at the moment.

"Are you still there?"

"Yes, Ma'am. Did you say, 'cake?'"

"You sure you're still there?"

"I'm sure. What kind of cake do want me to get?"

"It doesn't matter. It's for the family doings Saturday. Get one on sale if they have any."

The Twilight just won a round.

"Are you paying attention, Jimmy?"

"Yes, of course, Aunt Emma. It's just I thought you'd be baking one of your cakes like you always do. You know, from the old recipe book."

"I do believe you *are* getting a touch daft. Only a fool would bake a cake from scratch in this day and age."

I let it all sink in, but something didn't sound right. Not even in The Twilight Zone. "But what about all those great cakes you always bring to the family gatherings?"

"Come from the same place everybody else gets them, the grocery store."

"Then why do your cakes look and taste so much better than everybody else's?"

"Prettier plate, silly boy. Now are you going to get a cake for me or not?"

"Yes, Aunt Emma. But if everybody gets their cake at the same

135

place, why do they only ooh and ah over yours?"

"They do that to humor me. And I let them."

I gently put my phone in my pocket, turned the pan with the yolks in it upside down on the table, and reached for my first large trash bag.

End

THE NUTCRACKER

Oog did not have the appearance of a prehistoric trendsetter. It wasn't because he was short, or he lacked good looks—world history is full of ugly half-pint leaders. He was simply a dim bulb in a society whose members got out of the rain only by accident.

He spent most of his time with Og, a rather quiet cave guy, and Ug, a rather fetching cave gal. Those were not their real names of course. They had yet to develop vocal communication skills. *Oog* is what Oog uttered whenever he looked at Og. *Og* is what Og usually uttered whenever he looked at Ug. *Ug* is what Ug uttered whenever she looked at either Oog or Og.

These three survived nighttime dangers other cave folk often succumbed to, due to their interactions with each other. Og was afraid to sleep too soundly in case Oog tried to make a romantic move on Ug. Oog fidgeted throughout the nights about all the bewildering images that appeared in his head, which reinforced Og's paranoia. And Ug was apprehensive about the action, motives, and state of mind of them both.

They maintained such a constant state of hypertension over each other during the nights, and produced so much grunts, groans, and moans it frightened away any would-be predator.

This tiny group's survival success in the light of day was due to much of that same interaction with each other—except Oog's bizarre behavior increased while he was awake.

In contrast to Oog's hustle and bustle, Og preferred a more laid-back approach. His life was harsh, but simple enough even a dullard like himself could understand without any deep thoughts. This was fortunate, since all he cared about was a hearty meal from a berry bush, a reasonable good night's sleep, and an odd thrill whenever Ug happened to bend over.

Og was not especially tall for a caveman. He looked even shorter than he actually was because he spent so much time bent over picking berries. Og was a regular berry aficionado. But technically, he wasn't a real caveman. It seemed the bears of his era also had a fondness for caves, and they had the winning argument when setting-up house—or caves as it were.

Oog was a bit taller, but it was barely noticeable since he also spent much of his time bent. His bent, however, was somewhat different from Og's bent.

Ug also ate a lot of berries, although she ate quieter. She wasn't as tall as either Oog or Og, but her posture was better as well as her hygiene, alertness, and mental capacity. And she had great legs.

Naturally, the three of them got most of their sustenance from berries. Oog, however, was not sold on the one-course meal. He was fond of nuts. This greatly complicated his life and set him apart from his companions, who carried out more simple daily pursuits.

Unlike a plain berry meal nuts required more sophisticated preparation. You couldn't simply bend over, pluck one off a bush, and pop it in your mouth. In the first place, nuts grew out of reach in the branches of very tall trees. This meant a nut eater must either climb up into the lofty branches to pick the delicacies, or in Oog's case because he was afraid of heights, wait until a nut dropped to the ground on its own.

Once a nut became earthbound the nut eater faced another staggering challenge. That, of course, was to remove the hard shell in order to feast upon the meat of the nut. With age, a nut would eventually open by itself and was looked upon by Oog as a *stale* nut. Occasionally a nut would be found cracked open, but was not yet stale. This kind of nut he thought of as a *good eating* nut. A nut found on the ground without entering either state was considered by everyone simply as a *nut* nut.

As one would imagine the *stale* nuts far outnumbered the *good eating* nuts, and the *nut* nuts seemed to be everywhere. But The Age of Tools was not yet upon his kind and nutcrackers lay far in the future. No one was more aware of this cruel series of events than Oog.

Oog would stand around for hours and wish for more of the good eating nuts. This would frequently wear him out to the point he would collapse near a berry bush and not even bother to gorge himself on the plentiful repast at his fingertips.

Ug, being the more cautious and pragmatic of the breed, had noticed Oog's rather unusual behavior and kept her distance. But she also kept her eye on him. She had no idea why she bothered.

Og could not have cared less about Oog during the day, even though he did take delight in some of Oog's bewildering behavior at times. He had no idea why such things amused him.

The day eventually came when Oog graduated from the passive role of merely looking, and developed an active role of physically searching for the good eating nuts. This was an intellectual feat of momentous proportions, and things came close to getting out of hand numerous times before they actually did.

Oog's sudden burst of activity gave him a ferocious appetite, and his brain began to send him a continuous stream of perplexing messages.

Ug maintained a little more distance from Oog, but she still kept a watchful eye on him for reasons she could not quite fathom.

Og glanced up from his berry bushes from time to time to make sure he didn't miss anything, although he couldn't imagine what could possibly happen.

As time went by, Oog became more and more animated with his new interactive role. This made Ug more and more apprehensive, while Og started to see things he could never have imagined on his own. These were interesting times for them all.

Oog's first approach as a novice scientist was to physically hold a stale nut in one hand, a good eating nut in the other, and since he had run out of hands, placed a nut nut in his mouth. He had no idea why he did any of it.

Eventually, Oog tired of simply standing there and felt compelled to do *something*. So he began to chew on the nut nut in hopes it would somehow turn into a good eating nut without becoming a stale nut. But his teeth were not up to such a demanding challenge and his facial contortions gave Og considerable entertainment. Ug raised both eyebrows at the latest development in the neighborhood.

As strenuous as this experiment was, it yielded no fruits. Nor did it yield any nuts of the good eating kind. Even so, it did not discourage Oog from pressing vigorously onward in his great quest.

Oog next tried sitting on the nut nut. Then he tried to open it with his bare hands. He rolled on it. Spit on it. Glared at it. Beat his chest. Screamed.

Og was doubled over with guffaws. Ug was becoming frightened. Oog finally collapsed in exhaustion. The nut nut, having survived it all, remained a nut nut.

Some days later, Og pushed a large rock out of his way so he could get to a particularly delectable berry bush. The rock rolled down a slight incline onto a newly fallen nut, which promptly cracked open. None of this escaped the bleary stare of nearby Oog.

He failed to notice the birth of rock and roll, and because speech and vacuum cleaners had yet to come along, he didn't yell out *Eureka*! Instead, with great excitement, he rushed over with a fresh nut nut and carefully placed it on the ground next to the rock.

Because the rock was rather large, Oog had a terrible time trying to lift the thing. But he was determined. There was a lot of doubt in his mind about the rest of life's mysteries, but he was damn sure about the one he was working on now.

He eventually managed to lift the rock off the ground, but lost his grip and it crashed down on his bare foot. His expression of surprise and loud exclamation of considerable pain prompted Og to roar with uncontrollable laughter at Oog's misfortune. Ug, who somehow knew enough to be nearby in case of something like this, reacted in her own way.

So it was that civilization was enlightened threefold that day.

Ug rushed to the fallen Oog and caressed his bruised foot, which lessened his throbbing pain and placed him forever in her debt. This, she somehow knew, was to be the lot—or bane—of her kind from this time hence.

Og rolled on the ground, convulsed in laughter and gasping for breath. Through Oog, Og had discovered the standup comedian.

All the while, Oog, savoring the attention of Ug, realized he had developed a sure fire method to attract chicks.

End

THE MARS PROJECT

Evidently, there are many folks willing to give up their wretched life here on Earth for an even more wretched life on Mars. NASA found this out when it asked for volunteers to take a one-way trip to the Red Planet. The response was overwhelming. What follows here are previously un-classified records of how NASA got that first all-expense-paid trip off the ground and on its way to Mars.

THE REQUEST LETTER

Dear NASA,

I'd like to apply for your one-way trip to Mars. From the magazine articles I've read about the Red Planet, I feel I am as qualified as anybody else. Maybe more so.

For one, I haven't wasted my time getting in shape for the trip. As any fourth-grader can tell you, the gravity up there is only about a third as much as down here. That means I'm already three times stronger than any Earthling once I set foot on Mars. So, I could easily free anyone trapped under a Volkswagen up there by lifting the car all by myself.

Since I've forewent any muscle building program, my mind has been free to think about more important stuff. Like how to switch from a life on Earth to one on the Red Planet. To begin with, I kicked the fast food habit. Except for the fries. But I figure there will be a reasonable substitute for them by the time we lift off. If not, a big supply of chips would work since they weigh practically nothing. Even less on the trip through outer space. The rocket fuel needed to haul them wouldn't be much. I'd even be willing to chip in for the extra gas to get them there.

To earn my keep, I bring a bunch of work experience. I've been a vacuum cleaner salesman, house painter, dog groomer, assistant fry cook, and tree trimmer, just to name a few. (A complete work history can be provided on request.)

But that's not all I can bring along. We're all going to need a little entertainment in our time off on Mars. Now I'm no Justin Barber or Elton Johnny, but I play a pretty mean accordion. And my kazoo riffs are real show stoppers.

"I write my own songs so nobody knows if I'm doing them right or wrong." That's just a sample of one of my funny lines as a standup comedian. And another one, "I'm a regular Johnny Carson, but with a real golf club. . .and no TV camera." That one always cracks everybody up. I've got a million of 'em.

To fill in for me whenever I take a short vacation there, I have a VHS tape collection of movies and TV shows I've recorded off and on over the years. There are some real classics on those tapes, like Gilligan's Island, Lost in Space, and Star Trek.

As far as being able to get along with others, I have a whole bunch of Facebook friends. I'm even on a first name basis with the pizza delivery guy and my apartment manager. The lady at the Burger Emporium smiles at me, and the mailman always *waves when I honk at him.*

I know you won't be sorry to take me along, so see you on the launch pad, NASA, and then it's up, up and away!

Your Good Buddy,
Roger (Willy) Whirling

PS
Pretty please NASA, give me a shot at this. And let me know something before my apartment lease is up next month.

THE PHONE INQUIRY

"Good morning. Mars Project, how may I direct your call?"

"I'm really not sure. You see I sent a letter last week–"

"Oh, I'll connect you with our mail department."

"Mail room. Gus here."

"Uh, I don't think you can help me."

"Why? You don't think I know my job?"

"I'm sure you do, but you see I sent a letter last week and–"

"Yeah, and you want me to find out if it got here, right?"

"If it wouldn't be too much trouble."

"Hey, no trouble at all, buddy. All I have to do is wade through about half a million other letters to find it."

"Great. My name is Roger Whirling. Most people just call me Willy, but I used Roger on the envelope. It shouldn't be too hard to spot. I drew a big happy face on it."

"Nope. Don't see it."

"You looked already?"

"See how good I know my job? Bye now."

145

"No wait. Wait. Hello? Hello?"

"Good morning. Mars Project, how may I direct your call?"

"Well, maybe I could talk to somebody in reservations."

"I'll connect you."

"Bureau of Indian Affairs, how may I help you?"

"I'm sorry. I got the wrong number."

"Good morning. Mars Project, how may I direct your call?

"Hi, it's me again."

"Do I know you?"

"I don't think so. I'm Roger Whirling, but my friends call me Willy, and I sent you a letter–"

"How did you get my address? Are you stalking me?"

"No, no. I just want to go to Mars."

"Oh. You're sure you aren't stalking me?"

"I swear I'm not. I just–"

"I have to be careful about things like that, you know. Especially living all alone at 1442 East Magnolia Street, Apartment 118."

"Uh, okay. But I just want to go to Mars."

"You're sure?"

"I've always wanted to go. Ever since I was a little kid."

"Well, if you insist. I'll connect you to the Expedition Department. You did write down that address didn't you? I mean, in case you change your mind about going."

"What. . .Oh, yes. I did."

You have reached the Expedition Department. Please listen carefully, since our menu has changed. If you wish to continue in English, press one now. If you wish to continue in Arabic–

"I need to talk to someone about my letter."

To reach the Budget Department, press three-six-two. To reach the—

"Hello? Hello? Is anybody there?"

To reach the Cafeteria press—

"Is there a human I can talk to?"

To reach the Parking Garage—

"Please, anybody?"

To reach the Reservations Department, press Pound, Star, eight, eight—

"Oh, why not."

"Bureau of Indian Affairs, how may I help you?"

"Well, you might be more help than I've got so far. Do you have anyone there going to Mars?"

"No, but we strongly encourage the White Man to go there."

"Okay. I'm a White Man. How do you suggest I go about doing that?"

"Simple. Just write NASA a letter and tell them you want to go."

THE PROJECT COORDINATOR

Edward B. Bonifield sat behind a mountain of envelopes on his desk and sighed. It looked like a New York City post office at midnight on April the 15th. He simply could not understand why so many people wanted to go to Mars. Was life outside Houston really getting that bad?

Jean's voice came over his intercom. "Somebody here to cheer you up, Mister Bonifield."

Dave walked in and spread out in his favorite chair. "How's it going, Eddy?"

"Terrible. The latest budget cut took away my secretarial pool.

147

Now Jean has to double as my receptionist and my secretary."

"Think that's bad? It took away two of my propulsion engineers."

"Oh c'mon, Dave. Everybody knows you've had those rocket engines perfected for years."

"Everybody around Houston here. Not in Washington, though."

Bonifield sighed and ran his fingers through the pile of letters.

"Geez, Eddy, they take away your cleaning lady, too?"

"No, thank God. But without my secretarial pool, I don't have anybody to sort through this mess."

"Get Jean to help you."

"She refuses to have anything to do with it. Besides, she stays busy giving out excuses why I can't answer the phone. Can't afford to take her away from that."

"Do what I do with my mail."

"What?"

"I got a rubber stamp and had my secretary stamp every letter coming in that doesn't look like it might have a check in it."

"What's it say?"

"Wrong Department."

"But I can't do that with these letters." Bonifield held up one of the envelopes. "See? Every one of them has Mars Project Coordinator printed on them." He picked up several more for Dave to see. "Every one of them!"

"Wow. Must be hundreds."

"You mean thousands. And I have to evaluate five hundred of them, give them physicals and psychological tests, then pick fifty out of those for the Mars simulation. I can't possibly read so many letters, much less evaluate them and do any kind of tests. What am I going to do?"

"Well, first thing I'd do is stop crying. You have to do *something* with them. No sense in having to deal with soggy ones on top of that."

"You're right. But help me out here, Dave. You're an engineer. You're used to solving problems. I'm a bureaucrat. I never have to solve problems."

"Hum. I can think of one way, but it's pretty drastic."

"I'm desperate enough for drastic. Pretty or otherwise."

"Okay. You say there are over a thousand letters here?"

"Way over."

Dave pulled a blue and white device from his pocket, looked at the pile of letters, and used his thumbs to make numerous entries. In a matter of moments, he announced, "Alright, here's a way to get you through all this in time to take me to lunch."

"Really?"

"Really. You have a good shredder?"

"Of course. Every bureaucrat is issued one."

"Fine. All you have to do is shuffle the letters around a bit, count out 500 of them and put them in a drawer. Then shred the rest."

"You make it all sound so simple."

"Yeah, I know. Now take me to lunch before the end of Happy Hour."

OFFICIAL NOTIFICATION

Dear MR. ~~MRS. MISS. MS~~ WHIRLING

We are happy to announce that after careful and painstaking review you have been personally selected as one of the 500 semi-finalists for the Mars Expedition.

Roy L Cover

We will contact you soon for further testing in our meticulous process of picking fifty of the most qualified applicants for the final test before assigning twenty volunteers to become the first Martian Colonists.

Sincerely,

(signed)
Edward B. Bonifield
Mars Project Coordinator
National Aeronautics and Space Administration (that's NASA)

FIVE HUNDRED WANNABEES

The only sounds in Edward B. Bonifield's office were his dejected sighs from time to time until his secretary's voice came over the intercom.

"Mister Bonifield, are you available? There's a call from the president."

"Which one, Jean?"

"Ours."

"The president of NASA? Of course I'm—"

"Of the United States."

"Oh. I'm not here."

"But he wants to congratulate you on moving the program along so well."

"It's way too early in the day to congratulate me on anything. Tell him I'm in the can. No, wait. Don't tell him that. Tell him I'm in the middle of interviewing the Mars applicants."

"Should I tell him you will call him back when you're finished?"

"Good idea. I'll call him. Tell him not to call back. No, *ask* him to not bother calling here till I've finished with the interviews. Can you make it sound respectful, and groveling?"

"Of course. Anything else?"

"Yes. Call Dave and tell him I desperately need him. Now. Then rip the phone out of the wall and get in here."

Bonifield got up and paced back and forth, trying unsuccessfully not to look at his latest problem piled on his desk.

Jean walked in a few minutes later carrying her desk phone under her arm. Six feet of cord trailed along behind her. "Dave is on his way."

Bonifield looked up and blinked several times. "What are you doing with the phone?"

"You said to rip it out of the wall."

"Yes, but I. . .never mind." He sat back down and spread his arms to encompass the stacks of unopened envelopes on his desk. "I need help with all these."

"What are they?"

"What's left of the thousands of requests from the wannabe Martians."

"Oh."

"That's all you can say?"

"It's all I thought was appropriate."

"Well, how about saying something like, 'What can I do to help?'"

"What makes you think I can help?"

"I don't know. There must be something."

"I can't think of a thing."

"Well, arrange them in alphabetical order. Maybe it'll help."

"What are you going to do?"

"Do my level best to think up some questions to ask Dave when he gets in here."

"What would you do if his office wasn't across the hall?"

"Make friends with *whoever* was across the hall."

Jean picked up a stack of envelopes and began to place them into four separate stacks.

"What kind of sorting is that?" he asked.

"It isn't actually sorting," she answered. "I'm just re-stacking them according to size."

"What good will that do?"

"About as much good as sorting them in alphabetical order, I suppose."

It wasn't long before Dave made his usual jaunty entrance. "Good morning Eddy. Jean. What's our latest catastrophe in the Mars Project?"

Bonifield wondered why the man walked, and didn't just go ahead and skip wherever he went. He was so damn cheerful all the time. But he could solve problems.

"Dave, thank God you got here."

"It's only been five minutes since Jean called me," he said as he dropped into the chair in front of the desk.

"That long? Well, the important thing is you're here now."

"And your latest dilemma?"

"Picking fifty finalists out of these five hundred wannabees."

"Sounds simple enough to me. You don't see the solution?"

"It's my training, Dave. You were trained to solve problems. I was trained to look like I was solving things without actually changing anything. You know, don't rock the boat kind of thing. But my boat is not only rocking here, it's taking on water like a politician takes on lobbyists."

"Buy me lunch again?"

"I'll buy you more to drink than that."

"Deal. Remember how you picked the five hundred in the first place?"

"Yes."

"Do the same thing now, only pick every tenth person."

"I can't do it like you do."

"Why not?"

"Because I have to show NASA the applicants went through physicals and mental evaluations. And, the ones not picked would be looking for a lawyer if they thought somebody was picked without that kind of screening."

"Hold on a minute, Eddy," he said while he reached into his pocket.

"Why do you always bring out your calculator to address problems?"

"Oh, this isn't a calculator. It's a cell phone. I'm just texting my girlfriend."

"Tell her I said 'Hi,' Dave."

"Okay, Jean."

"Can we get back to my problem here?"

"Sure, Eddy. Let me see if I got this right. All fifty of the wannabee Martians have to have a physical before they can be approved for the mission, right?"

"Right."

"Okay. Now, even with your budget cuts, you should be able to afford a general practitioner to give fifty or sixty people a" regular checkup, right?"

"I think my budget can handle that, but we're dealing with five hundred, not fifty or sixty."

"Don't get ahead of me, Eddy. All we have to do is make sure you have at least fifty people who are physically fit. The rest could be shuffled through the way the Army did when they used to draft people. You know, 'If you can stand up, you're a private. If you can stand up straight, you're an officer.'"

"They used to do that?"

"If they didn't, they missed a golden opportunity. It would've really simplified things."

"Think we could do it here? I mean without the officer part?"

"Don't see why not. Once you have fifty healthy people, you can use some other way to make it look like the others are getting a regular physical."

"What other way is there?"

"I don't know yet. But there has to be a way. Any ideas, Jean?"

She stopped re-stacking envelopes and answered without hesitation, "Gregslist."

"Of course."

"What," Bonifield asked, "is a Gregslist?"

"Get with it, Eddy. Gregslist is the online site where you can find anything you want."

"Anything?"

"And then some," Jean answered.

Bonifield sat up straight and smiled. "Then my problem is solved."

Dave and Jean exchanged glances of disbelief.

Bonifield's smile faded as he noticed their expressions. "There must be a catch, huh?"

"The only catch," Dave answered, "is you need to know what you're looking for."

"Haven't you been paying attention, Dave? We're looking for a *solution* to my problem."

"Oh, is that all? It slipped my mind for a moment there. Jean, think you can find a solution for sale, cheap, on Gregslist?"

"New or used?" she asked with a grin.

"All right, you two," Bonifield pleaded. "Can we get serious here?"

Dave got up and walked around the desk and patted Bonifield's shoulder. "Sorry, Eddy. I just got a little carried away. Let's go over what we have so far." He paced around the office as he talked. "We need to have fifty people physically fit, and we have enough in your budget to hire a doctor to check them out. That part we can do, right?"

Bonifield nodded.

"Next, we need to make sure the rest of the applicants get a physical of one kind or another, so they can't complain. Right?"

"Depends on how many different kinds of physicals there are, I guess," Bonifield answered.

"Jean can find that out on Gregslist, can't you, Jean?"

"I think," she said, "I should get a little something out of all this extra work."

"How about lunch?" Bonifield asked.

"Not your kind. I prefer something more nutritious."

"Pizza?"

"Large."

"Deal," Bonifield said. "I'm beginning to feel like I should've opened up a bar and grill."

Dave continued, "Now we'll have fifty finalists, which will cover your—"

"Make that pepperoni and mushrooms," Jean said.

"You can do the ordering yourself," Bonifield said.

"If that's the case, I'll just wait and order it at home tonight. Wouldn't be able to eat it around here before it got cold anyway. Even if I could keep everybody's fingers out of it."

"We wouldn't touch your pizza," Bonifield said. "We go out for lunch."

"Uh, huh. But you never come back with a doggie bag."

"What do you think about things so far, Eddy?" Dave asked.

"I don't know. It all just seems to get more confusing by the minute. What about those psychological tests?"

"That's where we can disqualify as many of the original five hundred as we want."

"How do you figure?"

"Eddy, Eddy. We're talking about people who want to take a one-way trip to Mars. How hard could it be to show a few other cracks in their bell?"

"I see what you mean."

"Well, I need to get busy," Jean said as she headed for the door. "Not going to be easy to find a cheap doctor, even on Gregslist."

"Maybe there's some out there who'll trade their services for something other than cash."

"Good idea, Dave. I'll make a list and be back in a jiffy."

Bonifield cocked his head and stared at the departing Jean, then asked Dave, "Jiffy? What kind of word is that? And who uses it, anyway?"

"Your secretary does, Eddy. She even knows words like peachy, swell, and groovy. She's the bee's knees."

"I'll take your word for it. What can we do while she's doing all that?"

"Take me to lunch."

"You mean the bars are open this early?"

"Of course."

"Why hasn't somebody told me this before?"

"Some people just can't handle the truth, Eddy."

Two-and-a-half hours later they returned and swayed in front of Jean's desk.

She put her crossword puzzle aside and looked up. "About time you two got back. Can I go to lunch now?"

Bonifield leaned on her desk and said in a serious tone, "Don't bother. I think they're all out of peanuts." He looked over at Eddy and grinned. They both broke out in a fit of laughter.

"On second thought," Jean said as she looked at both of them, "I think I'd better stick around and keep an eye on you two."

"Peachy," Bonifield said. "Then you can hop in your jiffy and bring me that list of. . .of those things you were going to list." He and Dave laughed again as they staggered into Bonifield's office.

By the time their lunch wore off, Dave was stretched out on the office couch and Bonifield had slipped back into his gloom and despair.

"Dave. Dave?"

"Please don't shout. I'm just across the room."

"Then come over here and sit next to me."

Dave got up from the couch and moved a chair next to Bonifield. "I just hope the neighbors don't start to talk about this."

"They can't see. . .oh. How can you joke at a time like this?"

"C'mon, Eddy, you need to lighten up a little."

"I'll lighten up when I see that rocket ship blast off to Mars with those twenty wannabees on it."

"Don't you ever watch the news, Eddy?"

"What do you mean? Don't I have enough problems as it is without watching everybody else's problems, too?"

"What I meant was, twenty people can't take off at the same time in one rocket. They have to be sent up to the space station a few at a time."

"Why on Earth would they do that? Sounds like a lot of wasted trips."

"Not really. The ship going to Mars has to be built in orbit, because it's too big to take off from down here. That means a lot of smaller rockets from Earth to get all the supplies and people to the big rocket in orbit. See?"

Bonifield thought for several moments. "No. I still don't get it. And that's not my problem. My problem is to get fifty people tested, approved, and out of my life. I don't care how they go to Mars. Or what they do once they get there, for that matter."

"Not a very good attitude for a Mars Project Coordinator, Eddy."

"Well, it's the best I can come up with. I mean, how was I supposed to know we'd actually be ready to send people there when I wrangled my way into this job? I figured I'd be retired long before then."

Jean knocked three times and opened the office door. "Are you boys all the way back from your lunch yet, or should I come back later?"

"We're back all right," Dave said. "Can't you tell by Eddy's expression?"

"Oh yes. The familiar dark cloud of doom he's been wearing like a skullcap."

"Never mind what I'm wearing. Did you get that list?"

"Right here." She offered him several sheets of paper.

"Not me, give them to Dave. Then pull up a chair and see if we can figure this thing out."

Dave took the sheets of paper and looked them over for several minutes without saying anything.

Bonifield finally broke the silence. "Well?"

"There's a lot of possibilities here, Eddy."

"But is there anything more like, 'This is the answer to our problem?'"

"Possibly."

Jean smiled and said to Dave, "The asterisk in front of an entry means we might be able use it without spending very much money."

Bonifield ignored Dave's 'possibly' remark and leaned forward in his chair. "How many of those asterisks do you have?"

"Actually," Jean replied, "there are quite a few."

"Great. Let's do those, Dave."

"I don't know," Dave said as he flipped the pages back and forth. "Some of these things sound pretty far out."

"Hey, we're sending those wannabees pretty far out, too. I think we can afford to get a little far out with our solution here."

"Okay, how's this one sound to you? She found it on Gregslist, 'Witch doctor willing to provide services for used motorcycle. No Mopeds. Must provide transportation from Lincoln, Nebraska to job site.'"

"Are you out of your mind, Jean? A witch doctor?"

"Well, you have to give the applicants physicals. And this is a doctor."

"But. . .but a *witch* doctor?"

Jean insisted, "But still a *doctor*."

"Why not, Eddy? You need a real doctor to officially approve a wannabe Martian for this trip, but we're just trying to get rid of some of them. It shouldn't matter what kind of degree a guy has to un-qualify anybody."

Bonifield looked from Dave, to Jean, then back at Dave with his mouth open. He finally said, "Okay. But how do we get him a motorcycle and transportation down here without spending a lot of money?"

Jean spoke up. "My brother has an old motorcycle in his garage that has been there for years. I know he'd be glad to get rid of it."

"Does it run? Dave asked."

"What difference does that make?" Jean answered. "The ad didn't say it had to run, just be used."

"But," Bonifield asked, "how do we get him down here?"

Dave got up and stretched. "C'mon, Eddy. A little help here. There's an Air Force base there, remember?"

"Yeah, so what?"

"Simple. Tell the guy who runs the place to put doctor so-and-so of the Mars Project on a plane and send him down here. All official business."

"But what about the bone in his nose?"

"He won't even see the witch doctor. He'll just give orders to give the doctor a ride. The plane's crew will be the only ones to see the bone. I'm sure they're used to obeying stranger orders than that."

Bonifield was quiet for several moments. Then he got up, stood with his head held high, and clapped his hands. "You know, you're right. It's about time I started to use my official capacity for the good of mankind. Jean, first get a hold of that witch doctor and tell him he's got a deal. Then draft an official request on our most official looking stationary. Send it to whoever's in charge of those airplanes. And make it sound like I'm really important."

"No problem," she said. "I didn't take those creative writing courses for nothing."

"Moving right along here," Dave said as he got up and paced around the office. He looked over the other things on Jean's list. "All we need now is a psychiatrist or psychologist for the wackiness tests."

"Those guys make me nervous," Bonifield said as he sat back down and toyed with a rubber band. "They're always asking you questions. Are there any on the list that sound like they might not ask too many questions? And one who might work for free?"

Dave was quiet while he continued to read entries on the list until he suddenly laughed. "Oh yeah. Here's one who'll work free."

"I like the free part. Tell me more."

"Listen to this, 'State certified psychologist will psychoanalyze anyone in return for exotic expense paid vacation.'"

"Very funny, Dave. Who's going to spring for a vacation like that?"

"NASA. What could be more exotic than a vacation on Mars?"

"I think the phrase one way trip pretty much takes the word exotic out of a vacation."

"Picky, picky." He read several more items, then said, "Here's something we might be able to work with."

"Is it free?"

"As a matter of fact it is. 'You may be crazier than you think. Are more and more people calling you daffy these days? Fill out our FREE questionnaire to see if they might be onto something.'"

"Who put out an ad like that?"

"Some place called Happy Daze Sanitarium."

"We can't let those wannabees just fill out a questionnaire. There has to be some kind of evaluation."

Dave stopped pacing and stood in front of the desk. "But that's the beauty of this thing, Eddy. This place even does the evaluation."

"And you said it was free?"

"What it says here. But we really should get a psychologist guy to kind of oversee the questionnaire thing."

"Why do you want to ruin the perfectly good *free* part?"

"Because you want everything to look professional. The psychologist can hand out the questionnaires and kind of act like a school teacher. He can stand in front a group and say things like, 'Do your own work,' or 'No talking,' and 'Don't copy off your neighbor's paper.'"

"Then why can't we just get a teacher? They ought to be cheaper than a psychologist."

"Cheaper, yes, but we need somebody who can talk like one."

"Puts us back to the head doctor, huh?"

"Or somebody who can talk like one. Something might turn up in one of these other ads."

Bonifield sighed and turned his attention back to his rubber bands.

"How do you do that?" Dave asked.

"Do what?"

"That thing you're doing with the rubber band."

"Oh, just something I picked up from another bureaucrat. Helps to pass the time while I'm at work."

Jean entered the office with the transportation request. "Sign this, Mister Bonifield, and I'll send it special delivery to the airbase." She looked at Dave and asked, "How are things going?"

"Pretty good," Dave answered. "Might have our psycho problem solved from that sanity ad you got off Gregslist."

"The crazy ad? I just put it in there to give you guys a laugh."

Bonifield signed the request without reading it and handed it back to Jean. "Well, Dave thinks we could use it."

She raised her eyebrows and looked at Dave. "Really?"

"Yeah. I think it might work. But we need somebody who can talk like a psychologist. He wouldn't even have to be a real one. You know, just be able to throw a few psycho terms around now and then."

"Nothing chauvinistic about you, is there? What makes you think there aren't women psychologists around?"

"Actually, I hadn't given it much thought."

"I have," Bonifield said. "And frankly, it scares the hell out of me."

"You two are impossible. But for your information, I happen to have a niece who is going to college right now on her way to become a psychologist." She turned and headed out of the office, but held up the request letter before closing the door and said, "Excuse me while I give this to the mail-*man*."

"She didn't sound like she's in her jiffy anymore, Dave."

"No, and she doesn't sound too groovy, either. But she did give us some good information."

"About giving that request to the mailman?"

Dave stared at Bonifield a moment before answering. "Well, yeah. That was good information. But also about the part of her niece."

"Yes, I see what you mean. I, too, like to hear about young people furthering their education."

"How long did you say you've been playing with those rubber bands?"

"What's that have to do with her niece?"

"Nothing. You see, her niece is studying psychology, which means she knows some psycho lingo."

"You mean like, 'How does that make you feel?'"

"Something like that. Ask Jean to come back in here."

Bonifield flipped a switch on his intercom, "Jean, would you come in here, please?"

A moment later the door opened and she stepped into the office. "You beckoned, sir?"

"Jean," Dave said, "I'm sorry for those remarks. You're right about me. It's my upbringing. I'm just a chauvinist pig, and I deserve be to whipped. But I'm really trying to change. Honest. Forgive me? Please?"

"All those sweets, and me on a diet. Don't worry about it, Dave. I don't want to cramp your style. Now what is it you want?"

"Well," Dave cleared his throat, "you mentioned your niece is in college."

"Ah, yes. The psychological tests. What do you want the poor girl to do?"

"I want to do her a big favor."

"Sure. But go on."

"You know the ad you thought was a joke?"

"Of course. The chauvinist joke."

164

"Uh, yeah. That one. But all joking aside, Jean. If you could get her to administer some kind of test—"

"For free, of course?"

"No, she won't have to do it for nothing."

Bonifield jumped up. "But she can, can't she?"

"Now hold on, Eddy. All it will cost you is a letter to Jean's niece, uh. . ."

"Her name's Beverly," Jean said.

"Lovely name. Just send a letter to Beverly's professor saying she's assisting NASA in a crucial psychological phase of the Mars Project. If that isn't good for extra credit, I don't know what is."

"And what should I say in the letter about the assistance she is going to provide?" Jean asked.

"Say it's confidential. Top secret kind of stuff. She can't talk about it for seventy-five years."

"I suppose that could work. I'll ask her."

Bonifield fell back into his chair with a relieved sigh. "Had me worried for a minute there, Dave. But I suppose this will mean another sheet of that expensive stationary. How many of those do we have left, Jean?"

"Plenty."

"Those are the official ones with the fancy letterhead, right?"

"Right."

"Don't forget we still have to send all those wannabees another letter. And that means one to everybody who got picked to go on the mission, and also one to everybody who lucked out."

"We have plenty. This is the first time we've ever sent out more than one official letter a month since I've worked here. We have cases of the things."

"That many, huh? Think we could sell some on Gregslist?"

"I'll look into it," Jean replied.

Dave jumped up from his chair. "I've got it."

The sudden outburst caused Bonifield to lose control of his rubber band, which snapped out of his hand and smacked Jean's ear.

"Ow! Didn't you know that thing was loaded?"

"Sorry, Jean. What have you got, Dave?"

"The answer to our psycho tests."

"Let's hear it, I'm all ears."

"Just one for me," Jean said as she caressed her stinging ear.

"Jean can whip up a letter to this Happy Daze place on your very official stationary, and say they're needed for the Mars Project. Sound okay, so far?"

"Well," Bonifield said, "I haven't heard the word free yet."

"And I think," Jean added, "I need a smidgen more information before I start whipping."

"All right, make the letter sound like an official request from NASA. Emphasize national pride, duty to their country, and so forth." He glanced at Bonifield and added, "And put some emphasis on the free part in their Gregslist ad."

"Should be a piece of cake after all the other things I've been doing around here."

"What do I have to do, Jean?" Bonifield asked.

"You have the important job of applying your fancy signature to the letter."

HAPPY DAZE

D.D. Harbone sat at his large desk looking at the vase of daffodils next to the window. He couldn't make up his mind whether they looked parched or over-watered. Then he remembered they were plastic.

Rhonda entered the office and placed a half-dozen envelopes in front of him. "Good news in the mail this morning, Mister Harbone."

"We get a check from somebody?"

"No, but we didn't get any new bills."

He sighed and picked up his nameplate with the words, D.D. Harbone, Esquire– DIRECTOR, wiped it off, and carefully placed it back at the front of his desk. "I suppose that's something. Any of them have to be answered? You know, like ones that result in legal action if we don't?"

"Nothing like that, but here's one from NASA addressed to the director personally."

"What's a NASA?"

"National Aeronautics and Space Administration."

"Administration? National? That's a government thing, isn't it?"

"Yes sir."

"Well, what's it say?"

"It's marked personal. Don't you think you should be the one to read it?"

"Absolutely not. If it's bad news I can always say I never saw it."

She opened the envelope and read the contents in silence.

"Now c'mon, Rhonda, don't do that to me. Tell me what it says."

"Oh, boy."

"It says that?"

"No. It's what you're going to be saying after you hear this. It starts out, 'Your country needs you.'"

"Oh, boy," he said as he rubbed his forehead, "this can't be good."

"It gets better, 'As you are no doubt aware, NASA is

167

assembling a crew for a mission to Mars.'"

"How would I know something like that. Are they accusing me of some kind of classified information breach?"

"Not at all, sir. It goes on to say, 'To insure only the best America has to offer for a mission of this magnitude, we have selected your prestigious institution to provide a psychological evaluation of the volunteers.'"

"Prestigious? You're sure it's addressed to us?"

"No mistake, sir." Rhonda picked up the envelope and held it in front of his face. See?"

Harbone swallowed hard. "Get to the part where they ask for something."

"That's next. 'In light of your well known patriotism, and your eagerness to cooperate with the Government of The United States of America, the National Aeronautics and Space Administration officially requests five hundred copies of your free psychological evaluation questionnaires, as you advertised on the Gregslist website, to be sent to this office, and returned with your professional evaluation of each one in a timely manner.'"

"Oh, boy. And it says five hundred copies?"

"Uh huh. And it's signed, 'Edward B. Bonifield, Mars Project Coordinator, National Aeronautics and Space Administration (that's NASA).'"

"Oh, boy." He swallowed again. "How can I refuse anyone with a title like that? It's so much bigger than mine."

"Or refuse a country like that?"

Harbone sat for several moments rubbing his forehead. "This is not going to make someone very happy."

"Like Doctor Stevens?"

"Not like him, it'll be Stevens himself. Better get him in here. Maybe I can think of some way to break the news of all the extra work this means for him before he gets here."

Thirty minutes later Doctor Stevens adjusted his silk tie, checked his pocket watch, and winked at Rhonda before he opened the heavy oak door and stepped into Harbone's office.

"Ah, Doctor Stevens. Come in, come in. Please have a seat."

"Director Harbone. Always so nice of you to give me advance warning there is bad news afoot by addressing me as *Doctor* Stevens."

"It is? I mean there is? I do?"

"All of the above, Mister Harbone."

"Well then. I don't suppose there's any need for me to beat around in the brush."

"Bush."

"Huh?"

"It's, 'beat around the bush.'"

"Oh, of course it is. If you say so, I mean. You're always right about those things."

"Do you feel you are often wrong about everyday things with others?"

"Uh, no. I'm never wrong with other people. Just with you. I mean sometimes I'm wrong with others, but you're so smart. You know, educated like you are and all."

"You are not sounding at all like your usual self, Mister Harbone," Stevens said as he sat in the low chair in front of the desk, crossed his right leg over his left, and tented his fingers. "Why are you trying so hard to butter me up?"

"Okay. Let me just get rid of the brush, I mean bush, and put it in the lane–"

"You mean, put it on the line?"

"Well, I meant putting it in the lane we're going on here, but if you want it on a line that's okay with me."

The corners of Doctor Stevens' lips curved ever so slightly upwards. "We can go down that lane if you wish, sir."

Harbone took a quick breath and exhaled as he handed Stevens the NASA letter. "It's all in here. What do you think of it?"

"Interesting letterhead. I like all the stars at the top, and especially the little rocket ship in the middle of them. It reminds me of one of my patient's drawings."

"That nut didn't scribble on one of the walls again, did he?"

"No, of course not. You know I don't allow any of the residents to decorate the walls with their confused idea of art. I leave all those artistic decisions up to you."

"And I appreciate it. Now, what do you think of the letter?"

"It's very well written. Obviously composed by someone of high intelligence and good writing skills."

"Yes, yes, but what about the part that says it wants me to send them all those questionnaires?"

"Also well written."

"But what can I do about it, Stevens? I mean Doctor Stevens."

"I would suggest you either ignore their request, or honor it."

"Aren't you at all concerned about the extra work it would put on you to evaluate that many questionnaires?"

"Of course not. I designed those evaluations to be generic and apply to all but the most disturbed individual. Fortunately, that type would not likely volunteer to fill out the questionnaire in the first place. For the vast majority of participants, though, they will appear to have the ability to function in society under ordinary circumstances, but also have weak, or possibly strong, tendencies of abnormal behavior that may, or may not, develop into a spontaneous outburst of either verbal or physical actions that might, or might not, lead to undesirable results.

"The evaluation ends with a standard recommendation for a face-to-face consultation at Happy Daze if the participant has any questions or concerns about the results of the questionnaire."

Harbone sat staring at him for several moments before saying, "I see. But I don't know what any of that means."

"It means our evaluations are ambiguous enough for a layman to question whether or not he or she may need further psychoanalysis. The ambiguity also keeps us out of any court action."

"I understand the last part. But do you think all the other stuff will satisfy this NASA guy?"

"Indubitably."

"Huh?"

"Yes."

THE DOCTOR

A week after she mailed the letters to Happy Daze and the Air Force base, Jean carried a thirteen-pound box into Bonifield's office and dropped it on his desk. "I want a forklift if we're going to start getting packages like this."

"What's that?"

"The questionnaires from the Happy Daze Sanitarium."

"I meant a forklift, but I also meant the box."

"Then you got fifty percent of your questions answered. Get

Dave to answer the other fifty."

"Are you still upset over the remark he made about women psychologists?"

"Don't be silly. If I were to be upset over a stupid sexist remark, it would be something like you said about the idea of a woman psychologist scaring the hell out of you."

"So you're not upset, then?"

"Of course not. How could I get upset over anyone so easily frightened?"

"That's a relief. I forget how sensitive you women can get sometimes."

"I'll call Dave to come over."

"Good girl."

"Uh, huh."

It wasn't long before Dave breezed into Bonifield's office, overflowing with his usual high spirits. "How's my favorite Martian today?"

"Earthbound. And I have every intention of staying that way."

"Now, Eddy," he said and plopped into his favorite chair, "that's no way for a leader to talk."

"I'm no leader. I'm a bureaucrat. Let the leaders get out in front all they want. I'm perfectly comfortable right where I am."

"Which is putting together a hand-picked collection of America's finest to colonize Mars, right?"

"Who said anything about 'hand-picked?'"

"I think I heard it here in your office."

"I doubt it. Sounds more like something from some Washington bureaucrat. Those guys are so out of touch with reality."

Jean's voice came over Bonifield's intercom. "Doctor O'Reilly here to see you, sir."

Bonifield looked at Dave. "Do we know an O'Reilly?"

"I don't even know a doctor."

"Uh, Jean," Bonifield said over the intercom, "you know how busy I am right now. Could he come back tomorrow, or next week?"

"No, sir. She just arrived on a flight from Lincoln, Nebraska, and wants to talk to you about the motorcycle you promised."

Bonifield switched off the intercom. "Oh my god, Dave. That must be the witch doctor."

"A *she* witch doctor? Would that be a witch doctress?"

"Quit joking around. This is serious."

"Who's joking? Those witch doctors can do some serious things to a person. A she witch doctor probably can too."

"Like what?"

"For one thing, they can make a doll that looks like you and stick pins in it."

"That doesn't sound very serious."

"It is when you start to feel those pins in you, instead of in the doll."

Bonifield shuddered. "And I hate needles."

The intercom clicked again. "Shall I send the doctor in, sir?"

"Uh, give me a couple of minutes."

Dave rubbed his nose. "If I were you, I'd get that motorcycle for her. Quick."

"But Jean said it doesn't run. That might make the she-witch mad."

"I wouldn't be a bit surprised," Dave said as he got up and stretched. "Well, there's some important things I need to take care of in my office. See you after a while."

Bonifield jumped up and leaned over his desk. "You can't go now, it's almost happy hour. I mean lunch."

"Do I hear the old bribery ploy?"

"Yes, yes." He sank back into his chair. "For a whole week if you get me out of this."

"Okay. But you'll have to stall the witch while I go out and talk to Jean about the motorcycle."

"You mean leave me in here all alone with her and her dolls?"

"You'll be all right," Dave grinned as he headed for the door. "Just don't say anything to make her mad."

As Dave walked into the outer office he came face-to-face with the green-eyed statuesque witch doctor confidently balanced on a pair of black stilettos. She appeared to have been poured into her jeans with just the right amount to eliminate any wrinkles, but there was a generous overflow at the top of her peasant blouse. Flaming red hair cascaded down her back.

"Well hello-o-o there," Dave said after a slow up and down gaze.

"Are you my new boss?

"No, but I could be if you'd like."

"Then you'd better watch your tongue, buster, unless you want me to yank it out and tie you up with it."

Dave cleared his throat and turned to Jean. "It's okay to send Miss—"

"That's *Doctor* to you," the witch doctor said.

"Sorry, Doctor. Mister Bonifield can see you now."

"Thanks. And think of me if you ever want a budget colonoscopy."

As soon as she closed the office door behind her, Dave turned back to Jean. "What are you smiling about?"

"Smiling? I wanted to make it look more like a smirk."

"Just not going to let that little psychologist remark go, are you?"

"Not as long as you give me openings like that."

"Well ignore the openings for now. We have to help Eddy out with the broken motorcycle thing."

"Jean raised her right hand and snapped her fingers. "Consider it done, master."

"What do you mean?"

"I mean, Maggie and I talked over the phone before she got here. I just wanted to see how long it would take before my un-chauvinistic boss worked up his nerve to let her in his office."

"Maggie? *Maggie O'Reilly* is the witch doctor's name?"

"It's her given name. Her professional name is Mwanajuma."

"No comment."

"Wise decision. Anyway, I told her all about what kind of bike it was, how my brother stopped riding it a couple of years ago, and it didn't run. You know how we women are about talking."

"Should I be keeping score on how many digs you get on me?"

"You'd better. You know how bad women are with math."

"All right, I can see a definite smirk this time. So tell me how the motorcycle situation is fixed."

"She's okay with it. In her words, 'Ain't a hog in the world I can't fix in no time.'"

"That's a relief." Dave said as he turned toward the office door. "I'd better tell Eddy to stop sweating it."

"What's your rush?"

Dave stopped and thought for a moment, then smiled. "You're

right. I should give him and Mwanajuma a chance to get acquainted first."

Bonifield was furiously playing with a rubber band as Maggie strode into his office and demanded to know, "Are you the boss around here, or do I have to staple your lips together before you make some stupid remark like that bozo who just left?"

"I'm the boss," he answered as his rubber band sailed over her head. "I mean, I'm the coordinator of the Mars Project. And I don't have a stapler. Honest."

She settled into a provocative pose with one leg draped over the arm of a chair in front of his desk. "Fine. I'm Maggie O'Reilly, but since this is business you can call me Doctor Mwanajuma."

Bonifield rose, did a slight bow, and offered his hand. "Welcome, Doctor, uh, Mawa, Mawana–"

"Ma-wan-a-JOO-ma. Say it to yourself a few times. It'll just roll off your tongue. But do it later. Call me Doctor for now."

"Of course, Doctor," he said as he slowly lowered himself back into his chair.

"What do you keep staring at?"

"Your bone."

"What bone?"

"You don't have a bone."

"What the hell are you talking about?"

"The bone in your nose. You don't have a bone in your nose."

"You sure you don't have a stapler?"

"Positive. But maybe Jean–I mean I don't have one. I just thought all witch doctors wore a bone in their nose."

"Those are witch doctors in old Tarzan movies."

Bonifield relaxed a bit. "I suppose that goes for those scary masks, too, huh?"

"No, the mask is still part of my trade."

"Really?"

"Sure. You know, lipstick, eye shadow, a little blush. Sometimes I wear matching necklace and earrings."

"Of bones?"

"Gold when I can afford it. But usually just the costume variety you get at the shop-for-a-buck stores. What's with you and all these bones, anyway?"

"Well, uh, to be perfectly honest, you're not exactly what I expected in a witch doctor."

"How do you mean?"

"Gee, Doc, no–"

"Doctor."

"Yes. Gee, Doctor, no offense, but I kind of expected a black man with a bone in his nose. And here you turn out be white with no bone."

"And a woman?"

"Well, yes." Bonifield fidgeted as he stared at her sensual pose. "Certainly that."

"Uh, huh. Jean warned me about you. You're not going to turn this into some kind of gender discrimination thing, are you?"

"Absolutely not." He quickly looked everywhere around the room except at her while sputtering, "That's a positive no. To be sure. No sir. I mean Ma'am. Doctor. Magon. . .gunda–"

"Yeah, all right. She warned me about something like this, too. Just what is it you want me to do?"

"Yes, of course." He leaned slightly forward with his hands flat

177

on the desk, took a deep breath, and cleared his throat. "Down to business here. You see, as the coordinator of the Mars Project, I have to pick fifty people out of five hundred. Then send that fifty to a simulation camp where they'll eliminate all but twenty to go to Mars."

"You're putting me on, right?"

"No, no. they really want to go. All of them."

"So what's the problem?"

"They won't all fit."

"I thought Mars was bigger than that."

"It is. Or at least I think it is. But it's the rocket ship. It can only hold twenty, and I have to eliminate the rest."

"I still don't see the problem. Why don't you just point out fifty people and tell the others to get a life?"

"I have to have a doctor give physicals, so I can eliminate all but fifty of them."

"Huh. Let me get this straight. You flew me all the way down here, as a witch doctor, so you can tell a bunch of nuts they can't go to Mars?"

"Sounds a little crazy when you say it, but basically, yes."

"Would it help clear some of this up if I put a bone in my nose?"

He slowly shook his head. "I don't think so at this point. Let me get Dave in here to explain it all better. I'm still not very clear about the rocket ship thing myself anyway."

"You mean the bozo I met on the way in here?"

"That's him. He's my problem solver."

"Well this just gets better and better. Why don't you have Jean join us, too? And tell her to bring her stapler along."

Bonifield put his hand to his mouth.

O'Reilly smiled. "Just kidding, boss. She can leave the stapler on her desk."

"Jean," Bonifield said into his intercom, "would you and Dave come in here, please? But leave your stapler there."

Dave heard the intercom message and asked Jean, "Do you usually carry a stapler around with you?"

"I hadn't noticed. Maybe I should ask him."

"Not a bad idea. Might even think about filling out one of those psycho tests yourself, huh?"

"I think," Jean said as they walked into Bonifield's office, "I'd just as soon ask my niece about it."

"You mean, Beverly?"

"You actually remembered her name. Good boy."

They walked into Bonifield's office and Dave pulled two more chairs in front of the desk.

"What's this stapler thing all about?" Jean asked as she sat between Dave and Maggie.

"You didn't bring it, did you?" Bonifield asked in return.

Maggie smiled, put her hand on Jean's arm and winked at her.

Jean smiled back. "No, Mister Bonifield. But I left it out within easy reach in case I need it in a hurry."

Bonifield looked at each of them for a moment, then said to Dave, "Would you please explain a few things to Doctor O'Reilly?"

Dave looked across Jean at Maggie. "I'd be honored. What do you want know about?"

"First, skip the part about how you ended up with all these people who want to go to Mars in the first place. Just tell me why you don't want some of them now."

"Well, this is all a government project. Are you familiar with NASA?"

"Sounds familiar. Does that have something to do with stock car races?"

Dave thought a moment. "Come to think about it, they might. But this project is all about taking twenty volunteers to Mars."

"And to think I've been called a kook for being a witch doctor."

"But this has all been thought out," Dave said and picked up a model rocket ship from Bonifield's desk. "I personally spent over six years to develop the propulsion for a ship like this to take them there."

"And I spent over eight years to become a witch doctor. And I'm still called a kook."

Dave gave her a quizzical look.

"Of course," she continued, "not to my face. At least not more than once."

"You mean," Jean asked, "It took you more than eight years to become a witch doctor?"

"Oh, yeah." She took her leg off the arm of the chair and sat up straight. "You see, there isn't a regular school you can go to for something like that. I had to spend some time with different witch doctors all over the world. That's how I got into motorcycles. Cheap and fun transportation."

"So," Dave asked, "who awarded you with the doctorate degree?"

"Oh, I got that on Gregslist."

"Then, you're not really—"

"Of course she is." Bonifield interrupted. "Didn't you hear her say she has a degree?"

"I," Dave went on, "just meant—"

"You don't think I'm a real doctor," Maggie said. "Right?"

"No-o-o. That isn't, uh—"

"Sure it is." Her eyes narrowed and her voice dropped. "How about I whip up a doll of Mister Bonifield here and stick some pins in it? Would that convince you?"

"Yes, yes," Bonifield yelled. "I mean no. I mean that won't be necessary. He believes you. I believe you. Jean believes you. Don't you, Dave? Jean?"

Dave nodded first, then with a slight smile, Jean.

Maggie relaxed and leaned back in her chair. "Well that's good, 'cause I'm not into that voodoo stuff anyway."

Bonifield stared at her a moment. "But I thought—"

"Don't think so much. You draw too many wrong conclusions."

"Maggie," Jean said, "is the kind of witch doctor who doesn't hurt people. She helps them."

"Right, Jean," Maggie said, "but that's Mwanajuma. Maggie O'Reilly is still free to kick butt."

Maggie and Jean both laughed, while Bonifield and Dave sat in awkward silence.

As the laughter died, Bonifield cleared his throat and said, "Well, Doctor, if you still want the job you can start next week. Get with Jean to set up as many people as you want at a time for the physicals. Will you need any special equipment?"

Maggie grinned. "Like bones?"

The two women burst out laughing again.

"Of course. . .oh, you're joking. Ha, ha. Well, if there's anything you need, just ask Jean. You can use the room my secretarial pool was in. How long do you think it will take to examine all those people?"

Dave spoke before she could answer. "We could speed things

up by getting a nurse to check everyone first. You know, weigh them and take their blood pressure. Then all you'd have to do is ask a few questions to each one."

"What kind of questions?" Maggie asked.

"Eddy and I'll think up some for you."

"Well now, isn't that nice. You might not be as much of a jerk as I thought."

"I become less of a jerk the longer you know me."

"Yeah? Just don't push it."

"What," Jean asked, "do you plan to do with your time till then?"

"First thing is get that hog on the road. I figure it's something simple wrong, since your brother was riding it and then just let it sit. Probably a gas filter, or maybe plugs."

"Then what?"

"Set up a little work on the side in the motel I'm staying at. And this is my first time in Texas, so maybe a little sightseeing. Where do you keep those cows with the big horns?"

"They're Longhorns," Jean answered.

"Big horns, long horns whichever. Where can I see one?"

"Give me a call when you get the bike fixed and we can ride out to a place that has a few."

"Sounds good, Jean. In the meantime, is there a good bar close by?"

"As a matter of fact," Dave said, "Eddy and I were just going to lunch at a nice little place around the corner. We'd be honored to have you join us as our guest. And I believe they serve drinks there."

"And peanuts," Jean added. "In case you get hungry."

THE FIFTY

By midday Tuesday of the following week, Jean had turned Bonifield's office into the center of a well-organized project. The former secretarial pool room was now the official testing area. All the desks and file cabinets had been removed and sections partitioned off for each of the tests. The largest area contained two dozen classroom desks for filling out the Happy Daze questionnaires. A smaller section for the nurse held an eye chart, scales, and a blood pressure measuring unit. At the far end of the room, an even smaller area had been partitioned off for Mwanajuma's one-on-one interviews.

The Mars Project no longer even remotely resembled a bureaucratic operation.

Bonifield returned from lunch with Dave and staggered over to Jean's desk. "Did you say we're gonna start testing today?"

"I said," she answered, "Today, I'm going to notify the first batch of applicants when to come in for testing."

Dave leaned against the wall and said, "Told you."

"I know you did," Bonifield said. "But you were drinking when you said it."

"So were you."

"Only because I had to buy you lunch. And I wasn't gonna let you drink alone."

"You're a good friend, Eddy." Dave pushed himself away from the wall and opened the door. "But I've got to go to my office. Lots of work to do."

"Me too," Bonifield said. "Jean, I'll be on my couch. . .I mean in my office."

"Not so fast." She pointed at the five boxes on her desk. "You have to help me put names on all these folders."

He sat on the corner of the desk and searched his pockets for a pen. "No Problem. What name do you want on 'em?"

She looked at his bloodshot eyes and sighed. "On second thought, I think you would be more help on your couch with your eyes closed."

"Me too," he said and headed toward his office. "Don't disturb me if anything important comes up."

Maggie walked into Jean's office an hour later. "Well hi, Maggie. The motorcycle still running?"

"Like a rhino on steroids."

"I'll take that as good."

"You got it. Say," Maggie asked as she sat on the edge of the desk, "what kind of questions am I supposed to ask these characters, anyway?"

"You know, with all the other things going on, we haven't even gotten around to that."

"Well, since you seem to be the only one around here who thinks straight, got any ideas?"

Jean thought for a moment before answering. "I guess the first thing is talk like a medical doctor. Do you watch soap operas about hospitals, or any TV shows about doctors?"

"Don't even own a television."

"Okay then, movies. Watch some of those?"

"Now and then."

"Any of those have a doctor in them?"

Maggie thought back. "Yeah, a couple of them did."

"Good. Just talk like they did."

"One of the movies had subtitles."

"Go with the other one."

"I think that one had a proctologist in it."

Jean smiled. "No problem, they all use terms and language nobody else understands anyway. I'll work up a list of questions before you start interviewing."

"There is one more thing, Jean."

"What's that?"

"I've treated quite a few clients the last two days. You know, for expenses and a little walking around money, but they've been paying with chickens more than cash. My room rent will be due soon and I'm running low on funds. To make matters worse, the motel manager is complaining about the chickens."

"Don't you worry, Maggie, I'll get you enough money for everything."

"Not more chickens, though?"

"It'll be cash."

The next morning, Jean gave Bonifield a cherry greeting as he walked in and headed for his office. "Good morning, Mister Bonifield. Great day, isn't it?"

Somewhat confused, he stopped and asked, "Is this Friday?"

"Wednesday, but it's still a great day."

"Better than a Monday I suppose, but I wouldn't go so far as to say it was great. Maybe after happy hour."

"Oh, but it is great. Only three more working days before we start the tests."

"That soon? Are we ready?"

"Just a few minor details to take care of."

"Nothing you can't handle without me, though, right?"

She picked up a sheet of paper and checked off the items as she spoke. "All I need to do is talk with my niece and the nurse here in the building, then—"

"Nurse? We have a nurse here?"

"Of course."

"Huh. How about that. What's her name?"

"Ralph."

"You didn't by any chance mean to say Ruth, did you?"

"No chance. His name is Ralph. Quite a stud, too."

"And he already works for NASA, so we won't have to pay extra for him?"

"Right. We can scratch that one off the list for the emergency funds we need."

"Emergency? What emergency?"

Jean picked up a sheet of paper and laid it on her desk in front of Bonifield. "Why, this one of course."

"This is just a letter."

"But not just any letter. This is an official office copy of the ones I sent out yesterday. Go ahead, read it."

Bonifield picked up the copy and read,

Dear MR. ~~MRS. MISS. MS~~   WHIRLING

As one of the 500 finalists for the Mars Expedition, please come to our facilities in Building Three for preliminary tests at 8:00AM Tuesday. Be prepared to spend most of the day, so bring sufficient cash or a credit card to cover the cost of a snack in our upscale cafeteria. Or pack a lunch.

Sincerely,

(signed)

Edward B. Bonifield
Mars Project Coordinator
National Aeronautics and Space Administration (that's NASA)

He handed it to Jean and asked, "When did I sign this?"

"When you and Dave came back from lunch yesterday."

"We had lunch yesterday?"

"Quite a bit from the looks of you both when you came in."

"Now that I think about it I do remember signing something. I think. But how does this turn into an emergency?"

"Maggie is about to get kicked out of her motel, because she can't pay her bill with chickens."

Bonifield blinked several times. "I understand more about Dave's rocket ships than I do about what you just said."

"Maggie needs some money, so she can stay here to do the tests."

"Oh." He smiled and added, "Maybe we could put a tip jar in the exam room."

"I'll be sure to pass that along to her."

His smiled instantly disappeared. "What? No, don't tell her that. I've got a better idea. Get Dave in here."

"What's your better idea?"

"I just told you," he answered as he headed for his office. "Dave."

In less than ten minutes Dave breezed into the reception area. "You called, Jean?"

"His majesty is in dire need of his court jester, and I'm coming with you."

He smiled and made an exaggerated bow to her. "After you, m'lady."

"No way you're going to walk behind me. Get in there."

"Kind of early for lunch, isn't it Eddy?" Dave said as he opened the office door.

"I'm not sure. Do they deliver?"

"I've already tried," Dave said as he flopped into his favorite chair. "They don't."

Bonifield sighed and picked up a rubber band. "Jean, tell him about our emergency."

She sat in the chair next to Dave and explained the situation. He was quiet for several minutes while playing with his cell phone. Suddenly he sat up on the edge of his chair and yelled, "Yes."

Jean and Bonifield both jumped and asked, "What?"

"I finally out-scored the reigning champion in Zombie Kill."

"There seems to be no end to your talents," Jean said.

"Maybe I should congratulate you," Bonifield said, "but I'll save it for lunch. Right now I want to know how to solve this emergency situation."

"Nothing another week's worth of lunches can't fix, Eddy."

"Sometimes," Bonifield said, "it feels like I'm paying for your friendship."

"Not at all, Eddy. You're paying for my problem solving expertise."

Bonifield sighed. "Okay, you've got another week of free lunches. Now what's the answer?"

"Give her some money."

"That's it? Just give her money?"

"Simple, isn't it? I'm surprised you didn't come up with that one yourself."

"Just one question, Dave," Bonifield asked as he picked up a fresh rubber band, "where does this money come from?"

"The government, of course."

Bonifield lost control of his rubber band. "Are you talking about our government? Have you forgotten about the budget cut we just got?"

"Of course not. But you can always request emergency funds."

"Really?"

Jean leaned forward and said, "He's right. And this is an emergency."

He sighed and picked up another rubber band. "I guess they might consider it a minor one. How much do you think Ma-wa-jumbo is going to need?"

"With the funds you could get," Jean said, "I'd say you can afford to pay her at least a hundred–"

"Oh well, that's not–"

"Thousand."

"*What*?" Bonifield's jaw dropped to the floor. "A hundred thousand dollars? They're not going to give me that kind of money."

"You're right, Eddy," Dave said. "Nobody asks for a hundred thousand dollars in emergency funds."

"Well, I'm glad you're being realistic here. I was worried there for a–"

"Better ask for a couple million."

Bonifield's jaw dropped to the basement. "Have you gone insane?"

"No," Jean said, "he's right. The more you ask for, the less you have to explain in detail what you need the money for, and the less you have to itemize."

"But I can't possibly explain what I need that much money for."

"Think it would be easier to explain," Jean asked, "you need a hundred thousand dollars for a witch doctor so you can decide who goes to Mars?"

"Oh-h-h," Bonifield moaned as he put his head in his hands. "And just when things were going along so nice and smooth."

Dave leaned across the desk and patted Bonifield's shoulder. "It'll be all right, Eddy. All you have to do is tell the big boss at NASA you need a little more money to complete the evaluations."

"Oh, no. I don't ask him for anything, and he doesn't expect me to do anything. We have this leave-everything-the-way-it-is relationship."

"But what we're dealing with, Eddy, is not something you promised to do, or anybody here in Houston promised. This is something NASA itself promised. We're talking down-and-dirty politics here."

"But NASA isn't running for any kind of office."

"Of course not, but it depends on politicians for money, and politicians never stop campaigning."

"I still don't get it."

"Jean," Dave pleaded as he leaned back in his chair, "a little help here?"

"Not a chance," she answered. "Keep it up. I'm learning a lot here."

He took a deep breath. "Okay, Eddy, this is how it works. The media have recently stirred up the public about this mission. Especially with all those pictures Discovery sends back from Mars that seem to show everything from Egyptian mummies to empty beer cans."

"How did all that stuff get up there?"

"It didn't, Eddy." He turned to Jean, "C'mon, please?"

"Oh, all right," Jean answered. "Mister Bonifield, people want to believe there's intelligent life on Mars, or has been. And, they want the politicians to send some folks there to find out for sure about it."

"But the politicians don't have any rocket ships."

"Exactly," Dave said. "That's why they have to give NASA all the money it needs to send those Martian wannabes there."

Jean added, "And if the politicians give NASA enough money to do it, people will vote for them in the next election."

"Oh. A lot of that makes sense. But how do I get them to give some of that money to me?"

"Because," Dave said, "you've got them by the—"

"Throat," Jean interjected. "You're the one who has to put a Mars crew together. And, if you don't get some more money to do it, there won't be a mission. It won't be your fault you don't have enough money to finish it."

Bonifield concentrated on a new rubber band so long Dave thought he might have fallen asleep.

"Eddy? Any of that sink in?"

"Enough of it, I think. It seems downright unpatriotic if those politicians don't give me some more money. Why, why it would even be un-bureaucratic."

"Now you're talkin', Eddy. Get on the phone and tell your boss you need two million dollars immediately for unforeseen evaluation expenditures to complete the project on time."

"I'll do it. Jean, get Doe on the phone."

"Who?"

"You know. Doe. NASA's Director of Everything."

"Does he know you call him that?"

"Of course. . .not. And now I think about it, what if I can't spend it all?"

Dave grinned as he got out of his chair and headed out of the office. "Relax, Eddy, you're a bureaucrat. How hard can it be to spend a few million bucks?"

THE EVALUATIONS

Thursday morning Dave walked in and asked Jean, "How did Eddy make out with his call yesterday?"

She continued to write the names of the five hundred wannabee Martians on folders as she answered, "The big guy told him he'd think it over and call him back."

"Oh boy, I knew I should've given him some pointers on how to ask for money."

"Just as well you didn't."

"What are you talking about? 'Think it over' is bureaucratic speak for, 'Not no, but hell no.'"

"You know it and I know it, but Bonifield doesn't. He believes the guy is really thinking about coming up with the money."

"You don't seem too upset about it. What about the witch—I mean Maggie's rent money?"

Jean stopped writing and swiveled her chair to face him. "I wouldn't be a bit surprised if the money got here in time for her rent."

"Is that," he asked, "a smile or a smirk on your face?"

"Neither. It's mischievous."

Dave sat on the edge of the desk, picked up a pencil, and pushed it into the electric sharpener. "Care to let me in on it?"

"Sure. Before my glorious leader made the call, I drafted a short letter yesterday saying Bonifield will hold a press conference—"

"Eddy hold a press conference?" He inspected the pencil point a moment, then stuck it back in the sharpener. "He'd hop aboard a rocket to Mars first."

"Uh, huh." She took the pencil away from him and put it in a drawer. "But the people in Washington don't know that."

"And why should they care?"

"Because I wrote he will announce the Mars Project will temporarily suspend the evaluation program on Friday due to lack of funds."

"Wow. NASA is not going to like to hear him say that. They might even replace him."

"Oh, I don't think so." She smiled again. "You see, I emailed the letter to every member of Congress. They look on that kind of press release as a vote killer."

"What if it doesn't work?"

"It already has. I, or rather The Coordinator of The Mars Project, got an email this morning from the Ways and Means Committee. It allocated ten million dollars in temporary funds to tide us over until they can increase our budget permanently."

"Fantastic. Does Eddy know yet?"

"I thought I'd wait and let the big guy of NASA call and tell him. He needs to feel he's actually doing something around here. This way it won't come as such a shock to find out he really will have some things to do."

"What will he possibly have to do? I mean, he has a doctor, a nurse, and a psycho tester. All he needs to do now is sit back and shred stuff."

"Not quite. Maggie needs to have some questions to ask the

wannabes, so it'll look more legitimate."

Dave stood up and stretched. "Shouldn't be much of a problem for you two."

"Not a chance, buster. It's time you started to actually earn those free liquid lunches."

"What do you mean?"

"I mean you have nothing better to do anyway. And I'm sure you won't want to miss what Maggie wears while she's working."

"Oh?" He lifted his eyebrows and leaned on her desk. "What's she going to wear?"

"Sorry. Only members of the team are allowed in the testing area."

"Okay, I'll help out. But now I'm not sure whether that grin is mischievous, or a smirk."

"Neither. It's a gotcha grin."

"Before we start," Dave said as he headed for the door, "I need to take care of a couple things in my office. I'll be back in about an hour."

Forty-five minutes later Bonifield's intercom interrupted his rubber band routine with Jean's voice. "NASA's Director is on the line, Mister Bonifield. Shall I say you're in?"

"Should I be? I mean, does he sound friendly or mad?"

"I'd say congratulatory."

"You're sure he wants to talk to me?"

"He even mentioned you by name."

Bonifield put his rubber bands in the drawer, sat up straight, and took a deep breath. "In that case, I'm in."

Less than five minutes later, he forgot he had an intercom and rushed into the reception area and shouted, "Jean, guess what?"

"Yes, I got a raise."

His elation immediately turned to confusion. "Huh?"

"You left the intercom open and I heard the good news about the new money. Naturally, I assumed you would want your most devoted, and only, employee to have a tiny piece of that ten million dollars."

"*Ten* million?' His confusion deepened. "I thought it was two."

"That's what you asked for, but you know those Washington bureaucrats can't think in terms that small. Even ten mil is only if they're thinking about the petty cash fund."

"But now," he whined, "I have to spend ten million instead of two. And you know I can't show a surplus at the end of the fiscal year. They'd think I'm not doing my job and replace me."

"Yeah, it's possible they could even kick you upstairs over something like that."

"Oh no." Bonifield leaned on her desk for support. "Then I might be expected to produce something. You've got to help me out here, Jean."

"Love to."

Dave walked in and saw Bonifield leaning on Jean's desk. "What's the matter, Eddy, heartburn?"

"Worse. I have ten million dollars to get rid of."

"Man, you seem to have nothing but bad luck."

"I know," Bonifield moaned. "Got any suggestions?"

"Well, you could stop walking under ladders, maybe get yourself a rabbit's foot. No, better yet, get the witch doctor to make you a good luck potion."

"Not funny, Dave."

"It got your secretary to smile."

"You mean," Jean said, "it made his new *Assistant Coordinator* smile."

Bonifield and Dave looked at her as if she had just produced an armadillo out of thin air.

"Why not?" she asked. "And with my new promotion will come my own office, a secretary, manicurist—"

Bonifield interrupted her with a series of, "But, but, but—"

Jean cut him off with, "This is where your luck changes from bad to good. . .Eddy. All those expenses will immediately shave off at least three, maybe four mil off the ten. And that will be every year, which will come in handy when your new increased budget arrives."

"What increased budget?" Bonifield asked.

"Why the one the Ways and Means Committee is going to give you—us—next week. It should be a doozy, too, if this temporary ten million is any indication of how badly they want to keep the project alive."

"How can all this be happening to me?" Bonifield looked at Dave. "Nobody was supposed to seriously think about going to Mars for at least another ten, maybe twenty years. By then I could already be comfortably retired in Montana." He looked back at Jean and added, "At least in Fargo."

"Well," she said, "it is happening to you. And you're going to need me even more after we get these first fifty Martian wannabees on their way, Eddy."

"What do you mean first fifty? And why do you keep calling me Eddy?"

"Last question first. Eddy is your name, and now as a fellow bureaucratic executive, we should be more informal. Don't you agree, Eddy?"

"I, uh, well. . . .Do you happen to have a rubber band in your desk I could have?"

Jean ignored the question. "The Project doesn't end with those first fifty wannabees. We're going to be testing and evaluating an endless stream of people with stars in their eyes. Or Mars on the brain, in this case. You are really going to need me."

Dave spoke for the first time since his good luck jokes. "You know, she's right, Eddy. With her as your assistant, you can sit back and let her do all the work—"

"Kinda like," Jean added, "you do now."

"Right," Dave continued. "Only now you'll have someone to blame if anything goes wrong."

Bonifield let it all soak in for a minute. "Well, we do have all those millions to spend. And who's better at spending money than a woman?"

"And one of the first things I'm going spend it on is a pink glass cutter."

"What do you want with—"

"Leave it alone, Eddy," Dave said.

"Just one thing, though, Jean," Bonifield said.

"What?"

"Can we keep things the way they are till after we get this first bunch out of the way. . .please?"

"Well, with your please, and a raise on my next check, you can still be Mister Bonifield. Until the new budget gets here. Then it'll be Jean and Eddy."

Dave slapped Bonifield on the shoulder. "Great. Since that's all settled, c'mon. We're late for lunch."

Jean sighed. "Okay you two. First thing in the morning, though, we have to sit down and come up with some medical questions for the wannabees." She looked at Bonifield. "And don't stuff yourself so much on lunch you can't sign a check for Maggie."

"Maggie?"

"The witch doctor."

"Oh, right," he said as he and Dave hurried out the door.

Jean called Maggie, Ralph, and Beverly and told them to come to the office for an update on their duties for the testing.

Ralph came in later dressed in his nurse's uniform of white pants and form-fitting short sleeve shirt. He was an avid body builder and the clothes showed the great success he had with it. The only way he could have looked any more impressive was to have been on a Marine Corps recruiting poster.

While Jean was telling him where he could set up his scales and blood pressure station, Maggie walked in.

"What's up, Jean?" She then noticed Ralph sitting next to the desk and gave him a slow up and down gaze. "Well, hello-o-o there. With candy like you around, I'd never be able to stick to a diet."

Ralph's cheeks were instantly ablaze. "Hi, uh. . ."

Jean helped him out with, "Ralph, this is our interviewing doctor for the Project."

He quickly got out of his chair. "Glad to meet you, Doctor."

"Just call me Maggie. And often." She slowly ran her tongue across her upper lip. "Anytime."

"I will. . .I mean, I'll call you Maggie."

She looked over at Jean and said, "Isn't he precious?"

"And not to mention," Jean answered, "those bedroom eyes."

"What do you do around here," Maggie asked, "besides making girls drool?"

"I, I'm the resident nurse."

Maggie looked at Jean again and grinned. "Think this would be a good time for a doctor/nurse joke?"

"I'm not sure," Jean replied. "How about it, Ralph, know any good doctor/nurse jokes?"

His cheeks blazed hotter. "Uh, none I can remember right now."

"Well," Maggie said, "be sure to come to me with it whenever you remember one."

"Yes ma'am, I mean Maggie." He then asked Jean, "You need me for anything else?"

"No," Jean said. "Just as long as you know where you need to set things up."

"I'll have everything in place Tuesday morning." He walked past Maggie toward the door while she slowly looked him up and down once more. "Nice meeting you, uh, Maggie."

"Nice meeting you, Ralph."

When the door closed behind him, both women laughed and Jean said, "That was fun."

"And don't forget appetizing," Maggie added.

Before their laughter had completely died down, Bonifield and Dave returned and made their unsteady entrance.

"Was that our nurse who just left?" Bonifield asked.

Jean put on a serious face. "Yes, Nurse Ralph."

"Looked like his face was all sunburned."

"Uh, huh," Dave said as he playfully elbowed Bonifield. "Maybe he's a redskin." They both giggled like ten-year-olds over a bathroom joke.

"How immature," Maggie said, then turned back to Jean.

"What did you want to talk to me about?"

"About what this gentleman needs to sign for you," she answered. "Mister Bonifield, would you please sign this check for Miss O'Reilly?"

He took a zig zag route to her desk and steadied himself with his right hand, while he fumbled for a pen with his left.

"Oh, never mind," Jean told him. "I'll sign it. Don't want the bank to think it's a forgery."

"Good. Good idea. You always sign my name so much better than I do anyway."

Dave's second attempt at grasping the door knob paid off, and he held onto it as he pulled the door open. "These late lunches always make me sleepy. I'm going to my office and catch up on some work."

Before he could leave, though, a pert and tanned young woman breezed through the open door. "Thank you," she said. "Are you Mister Bonifield?"

At the sound of his name, Bonifield looked toward the door and struggled to focus his eyes on the source. Both he and Dave stared at her without speaking. She was dressed in short cut-off jeans, flip flops, and a white midi T-shirt with red letters that spelled, *if I were U I'd ogle me 2*. Her blonde ponytail flipped back and forth as she looked first at Bonifield, then Dave, then Bonifield again.

"Mister Bonifield," Jean said, "this is my niece, Beverly."

"Hi!" Beverly said, and quickly flip-flopped her way across the room and offered to shake his hand.

Bonifield refocused his eyes, collected his thoughts, and slowly offered his hand.

Her bright smile dimmed at his slow response. "Were you

expecting someone taller?"

He blinked a few times. "Well, maybe somebody a little more psychologist-y looking."

"Would it help," she asked as her brightness returned, "if I wore glasses and a beard?"

After a slight hesitation he replied, "I think so."

Jean spoke up. "She'll be smartly dressed Tuesday when she administers the psychological tests. Won't you Bev?"

"Huh? Oh sure, Aunt Jean."

"Dave," Jean said, "this might be a good time for you to catch up with that office work you said needed to be done."

He nodded, took one more look at Beverly, and left without closing the door behind him.

"I believe you also have a few things to catch up with in your own office, Mister Bonifield?"

"Good idea, Jean. Goodnight."

After the two men left Beverly asked, "Is it always like that around here?"

"Only on the good days," Jean answered as she signed Bonifield's name on two checks. She handed one to Maggie and the other to Beverly, who looked at hers first.

"Whoa-a-a. This will pay for a whole four-year degree."

"And that's exactly what it had better be used for, Bev," Jean said.

"Oh, it will, Aunt Jean," she promised as she headed out of the room. "I'll see you Tuesday morning."

Jean called after her, "Don't forget to wear some decent clothes. And more of them."

Maggie was equally amazed at the amount of her check. "Excuse me, but was I supposed to pay my room rent with this, or buy the motel?"

"Your choice," Jean answered. "But if I were you, I'd invest in some more permanent living accommodations."

"You mean here in Houston?"

"Well, at least close by. It won't be long before we'll have another group of wannabee Martians to sort through after we send this bunch on their way."

"You mean I could do this all over again?"

"Sure. But you'll get another check just like this one."

"Terrific." She looked at her check again. "But what am I supposed to do with this one. I mean, I can't cash something like this at the local Stop 'N' Spend store."

"Just go to the bank in the morning and open an account. Tell them to call here as a reference. Then come back and we can go over some of the questions you can ask the wannabees."

"Thanks so much, Jean. I'll be here as soon as I'm done at the bank. Oh, and buy some feed for my chickens."

YES, BUT MOSTLY NO

It was almost noon Friday by the time Maggie finished with the bank, fed her chickens, and opened the door to the Mars Project office. "Good morning, Jean. How are you fixed for eggs?"

"Thanks, but I already had a muffin for breakfast."

"No," Maggie said as she sat across the desk from her, "I mean fresh ones. Now that I can afford to feed my chickens I'll be up to my ears in eggs in no time."

"Maybe later on. I managed to wring a few questions out of Bonifield and Dave before they went to lunch. I trashed some of most ridiculous ones. You'll just have to try to keep a straight face when you ask the wannabees the ones left over."

"No sweat. We doctors are all taught how to keep a straight face when listening to patients' problems. We just file away the funniest stuff in our minds, then recall it later when we can let loose and laugh our butts off."

"Are you serious?"

"Serious as an IRS audit."

"I'll keep that in mind next time I see my doctor. But for now," she handed Maggie the list, "here are those questions."

Maggie looked them over, smiled at many of them, giggled at a few, and laughed outright at a couple others. "Well, this is certainly going to keep me awake through it all."

"We came up with about two dozen, but you only need to ask each person about five or six different ones."

"Okay, then what?"

Jean brought out another sheet of paper and gave it to her. "This is your diagnostic form. Write down the question number from our list you ask the wannabee. I numbered them so you won't have to write out the whole question."

"I'm sure glad you took charge of this fiasco, Jean. I don't even like to think what it would've been like if your boss did any of it."

"Thanks," Jean said as she got up and poured herself a cup of coffee. "Want some?"

"Sure. Just black is fine."

Jean brought the cups over and sat back down. "We're still not out of the woods here, though."

"How's that?"

"Well, we can only approve fifty of the wannabees, so we have to disqualify the rest for one reason or another in case somebody protests."

"Seems to me just wanting to go to Mars would disqualify a sane person."

Jean smiled and stirred a spoonful of sugar in her coffee. "I'm hoping the Happy Daze evaluation will be enough, but I want your medical opinions as a backup just in case."

"Gotcha. So how do I do it with these questions?"

"Let's say you ask question number eleven."

Maggie looked at the question sheet. *How often do you see a doctor?* "How can you disqualify somebody over that?"

"Well, if they answer never, or hardly ever, you can mark down something like 'neglects health.'"

"What if they have regular checkups?"

"Hypochondriac."

They both laughed. Then Maggie asked, "How about number three?"

Jean looked at the question sheet. "Oh, yes. If they've had any childhood diseases. Well, if they haven't, they still might come down with something to put them at risk."

"And if they've had mumps, measles, and whatnot?"

"Then they must be sickly."

They laughed again. "Yeah, I get it," Maggie said. "Sounds like fun. What do I do with the answers?"

"The wannabees all get their own records folder at the beginning of the day. Ralph will enter their weight and blood pressure in it along with an eye and hearing test. Then they give it to you, but you keep it after asking the questions. Tell them the information will be reviewed by a panel appointed by the project coordinator, and they will be notified of the results in a week or so."

"And I imagine I'm talking to that panel now, huh?"

Jean sighed, "Yeah, I'm the panel, receptionist, and any other title that means doing anything around here. Which reminds me, I need to reaffirm the appointment for fifty of the wannabees for their physicals at the Cut Rate Clinic. Then call Rhonda over at Happy Daze before the boys get back from lunch."

"Well, I'll get out of your hair and take care of a few things myself." Maggie set her cup on the desk and walked to the door. "Hey, since you don't work tomorrow, want to ride out with me and look at some of those cows with the big–I mean long horns?"

"Sure. Sounds like fun."

Rhonda hung up the phone and keyed the intercom. "Mister Harbone, I just received some news from NASA. May I come in and discuss it with you?"

"Can't it wait? I'm in the middle of watching a mental institutions training film."

"It's very important, sir."

"Okay," he sighed as he took his feet off the desk. "But make it short." He sat up straight and turned off the movie, *One Flew Over The Cuckoo Nest.*

"Mister Bonifield's secretary just called to let me know their office is prepared to reimburse us for returning the first evaluation for their appraisal within a day after receiving it."

"Why didn't she let me know?"

"I'm letting you know now, sir."

"But why tell you and not me?"

"Because you never answer your phone."

Harbone spread his arms and leaned forward. "Of course I don't answer it. Never know when it might be a bill collector, or a salesman trying to get me to buy something."

"Well, that's the reason."

He settled back in his chair, but only for a moment. "Reason for what?"

"The reason she told me instead of you."

"I know she told you. What I want to know is what this reimbursement is all about. Why can't you people get it through your head this joint is supposed to make money?"

"It usually starts to soak in after about the eighth or ninth time you say it to me every day."

"How many times have I told you that this morning?"

She looked up at the ceiling while thinking. "I lost count. You'll have to start over."

Harbone swiveled his chair around and looked out the window while he drummed his fingers on his stomach for several moments. "You need to do something about that memory of yours."

He swiveled back around and faced her while he drummed his fingers a few more times. "I'll bet you don't even remember why I called you in here, do you?"

Rhonda smiled. "No, but I'll bet I have something even better you'd like to hear."

He pursed his lips and sat in silence for several moments. "All right, tell me what you think I'd like to hear. Then I'll tell you if it's more important than why I sent for you."

Her smile grew wider. "NASA is going to give us a bunch of money."

Harbone continued to stare at her without saying anything for so long she began to worry. "Are you okay, sir?"

He cleared his throat, leaned across his desk, and whispered, "Is it some kind of bribe?"

"Oh no, sir. It's all a legitimate business arrangement."

He settled back in his chair and took a deep breath. "Then by all means take their money."

"Don't you want to know why?"

"Get the money first. I'll find out later."

"Well, you might want to talk it over with Doctor Stevens. He's the one who will have to do the work to fulfill our obligation to the agreement."

He leaned forward again. "Obligation? I should've known there was a catch."

"It's not much. All Doctor Stevens has to do is return those evaluations by the end of next week. Then they'll pay us a hundred dollars for each one, and a hundred dollars for each additional one if we expedite them the same way."

"That's it? For five hundred thousand bucks?"

"That's it."

"Well," he exhaled and sank back into his chair, "what are you waiting for? Get on the phone and tell them cash is preferred. But we'll accept a check, money order, or credit card."

"Don't you think you should check with Doctor Stevens first?"

"He accepts, too. If he can't do those things by himself fast enough, I'll get the janitor to help him."

Tuesday morning, NASA's Mars Project had gone from a bureaucratic musical chairs to an efficient operation. Ralph took weight, temperatures, and blood pressure faster than a vegan can say no to a pork chop. As soon as he finished with twenty-five wannabees, Jean herded them into the psychological testing area.

There, Beverly handed out the Happy Daze questionnaires with professional-like instructions. They had exactly eighteen minutes to fill them out and lay down their pencils before she picked them up.

Jean then took charge again and told the group to line up in front of Maggie's small office for her evaluation. She looked over the top of her glasses at the line with a stern face and made a note on her clipboard. "Give your medical folder to the doctor when you enter her office and do not make small talk. Keep the noise down while you wait. Stop in the front office and check out with me before you leave."

Bonifield was duly impressed, though confused, over the transformation. His department now actually functioned, which was a foreign concept to him. He turned to Jean for support, but she was preoccupied keeping everything on schedule. Dave was no help either. He kept trying to catch a glimpse of Maggie in her short-short skirt and low cut blouse, but was distracted by Beverly's even shorter skirt and equally low cut blouse.

A few minutes before noon Jean announced, "Listen up, everyone. We're going to break for lunch. The cafeteria is one floor down. Be back here at one, no sooner."

Jean intercepted Bonifield and Dave before they reached the door. "Oh no, you don't. The cafeteria is sending up pizza."

"But," Bonifield said, "this is Happy, uh, Happy Lunch Hour."

"I'm well aware how happy it makes you both. That's why your lunch hour will be here for the rest of the week. *If* you want me to get these tests done."

Bonifield hung his head and turned away. "All right, we'll do it your way. But if there's any anchovies on my pizza I'm picking them off."

Jean watched to make sure they both went into Bonifield's office before she brought Maggie, Beverly, and Ralph into the front reception area. While they waited for the pizza she said, "You're doing a great job, guys. But it looks like Maggie is getting a little overwhelmed."

"Yeah, that's a good word for it," Maggie said. "I was sure I could get each one done in about two or three minutes, but they can't answer the questions fast enough."

Beverly spoke up. "Maybe we could type out the questions and hand them out before they see Maggie."

"Sure," Jean said. "That would give them time to remember past medical things. Pick out some of your favorite questions, Maggie. I'll type them out and make a bunch of copies to hand to the ones in line."

"Great idea," Maggie said. "What do you think, Ralph?"

Ralph tore his eyes away from Beverly long enough to reply, "Just great."

Jean and Maggie exchanged looks and grinned.

Before anyone else arrived at the office Friday morning, Jean made sure all the wannabees' vital statistics had been recorded by Ralph. Then she double-checked the postage on the package of questionnaires for Happy Daze as Maggie walked in.

"Good morning, Jean. Think we can wrap it up today?"

"Up to you. Ralph and Bev are finished. Only eighty-three left for you to see."

"Hey, piece of cake. Probably be done by lunch. Been rolling right along since Bev came up with the idea to give those people the questions in advance."

"And speaking of. . ." Jean said.

Beverly made her usual bouncy entrance with Ralph panting close behind. "Hi guys," she said. "Ralph and I were just talking, and since we're both done here, could we, you know, like do some other stuff?"

Maggie smiled and Jean asked, "Like. . .?"

"Oh, you know, like, see things around here."

"Like?" Jean asked again.

"Aw c'mon, Aunt Jean. We'd just be in the way."

"Oh, all right. But check back here before you go home."

"Thanks, Aunt Jean," She grabbed Ralph's hand and they hurried out the door.

Maggie looked at Jean and smiled again. "Like, I didn't know there was so much to see around here."

"Me either, but I'll bet they find something interesting."

Bonifield walked in and asked, "Where are they going in such a hurry?"

"To look for something interesting to see," Jean answered.

He thought for a moment. "Around here?"

"You'll be happy to know, Mister Bonifield," Jean said, "we'll be finished testing today."

He instantly looked like a television toothpaste ad and rubbed his hands. "Finally. Now maybe things can get back to normal."

"I'm afraid your idea of normal is gone forever."

The toothpaste ad faded and the hand rubbing stopped in mid-rub. "But you just said we'd be done testing today."

"And we will," Jean said. "But we still have to keep track of the final fifty when they go to the Mars Simulation Retreat."

"But that's way out in one of those desert states. We don't have anything to do with any retreat."

"On the contrary. We're still responsible to provide twenty people to board a rocket and blast off to Mars. So, if more than twenty people drop out of the program we'll have to replace them with some of the ones we've disqualified."

Like a third-grader living in a fourth floor apartment asking for a pony, Bonifield tried his own style of rebuttal. "That wouldn't be such a big problem, would it?"

"It'd be a mess," Jean answered with her more traditional logic. "The main reason for the simulator is to see how well the twenty wannabees can get along with each other. If even one new person is added at any time, the whole bunch would have to start over as a new group. The ones who had already been in there are not going to be very happy with the newbie making them do it all over again. We'd have to start with a completely different group."

Bonifield began to pace in front of her desk and accompanied his next questions with expansive arm and hand signals to accent his own logic. "Can't we just have another bunch on stand-by?"

"We have a deadline for a launch," she answered in calm voice. "There are only certain times a rocket can leave Earth and get to Mars in the shortest time."

"Who decided that?"

"Some astronomer."

"Well, can't he," Bonifield glanced over at Maggie, "it is a he, isn't it?"

Jean smiled and said, "I think so."

"Okay, can't he just make out a new schedule?"

"I doubt it. It has to do with the motions of the planets and things."

"Oh-h-h," he groaned as he quit pacing leaned against Jean's desk. "This is just getting more and more complicated."

"There is one thing we can do to make it less complicated, though."

He immediately brightened. "Why didn't you say so sooner?"

"Because you need to be aware of all this in case somebody asks you about it and I'm not around."

"Where will you be?"

"As close as possible, but sometimes you wander out of sight. Like at lunch time."

"A man's gotta eat."

"Uh, huh. I've read a few articles by some psychologists who claim twelve weeks in the simulator is probably more than enough time to find out if a group of twenty can get along."

"More psychologists? I thought you said this was going to get less complicated?"

"It is. If we end up with more than twenty wannabees at the end of twelve weeks, we just dismiss the excess people with some excuse and continue on schedule. But if the number drops to twenty before the end of twelve weeks, we stop the simulation exercise and give the remaining twenty some time off before the launch."

"I'm not following very much of this, but I think I believe you."

"You're in good hands, sir. It's all going to work out."

Bonifield slowly shook his head. "Whoever came up with this insane idea to actually go to Mars in the first place?"

"Hey," Jean said, "it's job security."

"It was job security when all they did was *talk* about going."

Maggie got up and walked toward the testing room. "Well, this has all been very interesting, but I'm going to get ready for the wannabees now."

"And," Jean said, "I have to compose some good news letters and some bad news ones."

"Does that mean," Bonifield asked, "I'll have to sign some things?"

"I'm going to have pity on you today, Mister Bonifield. I'll sign the letters for you, and let you go to lunch with Dave."

The toothpaste ad returned in full force along with the hand rubbing. "Really?"

"Really," Jean answered. "With you and Drooling Dave out of my hair I'll be able to tie up the loose ends in this thing."

"This is great. Those clowns down in the cafeteria wouldn't quit putting anchovies on my pizza. And I really miss my regular lunch specials."

THE LETTERS

Dear Mars Project Participant,

You did very well in the selection process, but after careful and lengthy testing and reviews, we are sorry to inform you that you will not be participating in the Mars simulation retreat for the final elimination test to determine the final twenty colonists.

This does not mean you were necessarily unqualified, it means only the field of volunteers was so large eliminations of numerous qualified people was unavoidable. However, NASA has plans for more Mars trips in the future, so feel free to volunteer again.

Thank you for your time, effort, and dedication to help make the colonization of Mars a reality.

Roy L Cover

Sincerely,

(signed)
Edward B. Bonifield
Mars Project Coordinator
National Aeronautics and Space Administration (that's NASA)

Congratulations   MR. ~~MRS. MISS. MS~~   *WHIRLING*

We are happy to announce, after careful and painstaking reviews, you have been personally selected as one of the fifty finalists to participate in the Mars Simulation where the final twenty colonists will be chosen.

You be contacted soon by the Mars Simulation Instructor with further instructions.

Sincerely,

(signed)
Edward B. Bonifield
Mars Project Coordinator
National Aeronautics and Space Administration (that's NASA)

WHIRLING:

GET YOUR ASS ON THE BUS IN FRONT OF THE NASA BUILDING AT ZERO SIX HUNDRED MONDAY MORNING. DO NOT BRING ANYTHING WITH YOU BUT THE CLOTHES ON YOUR BACK.

(Signed)
GUNNERY SERGEANT BREAKER, USMC, RET.
MARS SIMULATOR INSTRUCTOR

THE LEFTOVERS

Sergeant Breaker stood like a statue in his Smokey Bear hat and crisply pressed uniform as the bus stopped in front of him. He waited until all fifty men and women had filed out and nervously stood around talking among themselves.

Suddenly, he began to bark out orders, information, and personal observations in a rapid fire greeting. "Listen up! I'm Gunnery Sergeant Breaker, but you will call me 'sir.' I am not here to hold your puny little hands, nor am I here to read you bedtime stories. I am here to make sure you stay in those five connected buildings behind you until three months have passed, or the weakest of you bangs on the door in a panic begging me to let you out before then, which from the looks of this mob that should begin in about thirty minutes after you get inside. Everything you need to survive is already in there, so there will be no contact from me other than to rescue you from yourself. You will find printed instructions throughout the buildings such as you will find on Mars, if you are sufficiently capable of making it that far, which would surprise me to no end if any of you make it. Are there any questions?

"All of you with your hands up can put them back down. I already told you there are printed instructions in the buildings. Now everybody inside. Move, move, move!"

Within six weeks twenty participants had banged on the door screaming and pleading to be let out. The two married couples were gone before the end of the first week. By the end of nine weeks the field had narrowed to twenty, and Sergeant Breaker unlocked the door.

When the twenty wannabees filed out of the building blinking in the bright sunshine, the sergeant announced in his usual manner, "The powers that be have decided you twenty people are the best they are likely to get. You have now graduated from Martian Wannabees to official Mars Colonists. Congratulations. Yes, you with your hand up?"

"No, you will not be getting a diploma."

BON VOYAGE

"Welcome aboard the Mars Explorer. I'm Brad, your flight attendant. Technically, I am a trip attendant since we don't actually *fly* through space.

"For the duration of my little presentation here, everyone keep your seat belt fastened and your mouth shut. A silent nod will let me know you understand.

"Fine.

"Now pay attention, because I'm only going to go over this once.

"First off, now that we've left Earth's gravity, some of you may feel a little queasy. That's what those plastic bags on the back of the seat in front of you are for. Use as many as you need. Nobody wants to see pieces of your tuna fish sandwich floating around, or anything else you decided to eat just before takeoff—which, we told you not to do.

"You, back there with your hand up. Put it down. There'll be time for questions later.

"Our trip will be much more pleasant if everyone follows a few simple rules. You might want to write these down.

"Rule number one. Never, ever ask, 'Are we there yet?' We will let you know the minute we land on Mars.

"Rule number two. Do not ask to visit the cockpit. The computer keeps us on course, but the pilot still has to watch out for things like asteroids and other space junk that could damage the ship.

"No, Hal is not the ship's computer. Put your hands down.

"You there. Yes, you on the ceiling. What did I just say about your seat belt?

"You in the seat under him, grab his leg and pull him down.

"I don't know. Hold him in your lap till I'm done talking.

"Well ma'am, you knew there were going to be men along when you signed up.

"All right everybody, stop giggling.

"Rule number three. Your trip attendant is not your nursemaid. If you don't feel well, see the ship's doctor. If you want something, ask one of the other passengers. I have more important things to do than to get you stuff.

"Important things.

"Very, important things.

"Like making sure annoying passengers don't somehow fly out through a hatch into space.

"Which brings me to rule number four. Do not become an annoying passenger.

"Rule number five. Never try to open a hatch or port to throw something out. We recycle everything.

"Yes, even that.

"Didn't you listen during your indoctrination lectures when that was explained?

"Well, you should have. You might not be on this trip if you had.

"Rule number six. There will be no ball games, games of tag, or water fights in the recreation area.

"Because it is meant only for reading, chess, scrabble, and other mental activities, that's why.

"Rule number seven. No running. Ever.

"No, not even if you're on fire.

"Because we can't put you out if you're running away from us.

"Rule number eight. Do not touch the thermostat.

"Then put on a sweater.

"Now, are there any questions? Yes, you had your hand up earlier.

"They are not marked, because they are equipped to handle either men or women.

"They are equipped to handle everyone. Just slide the little occupied sign on the door.

"Anyone else? Yes?

"No, we did not forget to put an inflatable vest under your seat. It was a choice between the vest and a Wi Fi connection.

"Other questions? Okay, you.

"If it isn't in your carry-on, you'll just have to do without it till we're there.

"You're right. It will no doubt spoil before we land.

"Yes, you.

"No, your cell phone won't work out here.

"You're just going to have to deal with it.

"Anybody else?

"Yes, you can let him off your lap now.

"You are all now free to float about the cabin.

"God, this is going to be a long trip."

WRONG WAY EVERYBODY

Harry set the coffee cup down on his cluttered desk and picked up the phone. "Director's office, Harry speaking. Oh, hello Jean. How's the weather there in Houston?

"Well, it sounds better than what we're having in D.C. today. What's new?

"They're *what*?

"You're kidding me. How could this happen in just three weeks?

"Uh, huh. I see. Any other details?

"Okay. I'll let the Big Guy know. Call me the minute you hear anything new."

Harry took a deep breath and exhaled before he walked over to the oak door with the polished brass plate proclaiming, *B.T. Bradstone, NASA Director of Everything*. He rapped twice, then boldly made his way across the thick carpet and stood in front of the huge desk.

"Excuse me, sir, but there seems to be a slight problem with the Mars Project."

Bradstone put his rubber bands in a drawer and looked up. "What is it now?"

"Well, they appear to be lost."

"*Appear* to be lost?"

"They *are* lost."

"How do you know?"

"They radioed the message, sir."

"What idiots. How could they get lost? I mean how many planets named Mars are there out there, anyway?"

"Just one, I believe, sir."

"And they can't find it?"

"Evidently not."

"What do they want me to do, give them directions?"

"It may come down to that."

"Better get me an up-to-date star map. We have one of those around here, don't we?"

"I'll check."

"And better let the senator in on this. Don't need him to do something stupid like holding a press conference and not knowing what to say. And after you do that, announce I'll hold a press conference this afternoon."

"What will you tell them?"

"I don't know." He brought the rubber bands back out of the drawer and began a complex maneuver with them. "Come up with something for me to say."

Three blocks away, Martin answered the phone on the sixth ring. "Senator Tripper's office. Oh hi, Harry."

"Oh, no. For real?"

"What happened?"

"That's all you've heard, huh?

"Well, I'll tell him. If you hear a loud noise from over in this direction, you'll know he got the message."

Martin waited until the visiting dignitary left and entered the senator's office. He closed the door behind him, and said, "Senator, we have just received news the Mars ship appears to be lost."

"I didn't lose it, did I?"

"No, sir."

"Thank God. That would mean another congressional hearing.

Who do they say lost it?"

"I assume it was the ship's captain."

"How could he lose his own ship?"

"Space is pretty big, sir."

"So I've heard. What do they want me to do about it?"

"I think it was just more of a courtesy call."

"Giving me bad news in an election year? Who the hell thinks something like that is a courtesy?"

"It came from Director Bradstone, sir."

"And after I got the Ways and Means committee to give him all that money, this is the thanks I get? Bad news?"

"I don't think he did it on purpose, sir."

"What, lose the ship, or give me the bad news?"

"He didn't lose the ship."

"Can he prove that, or is he trying to make me a scapegoat in this thing?"

"Maybe I should try to find some more information about the matter, sir."

"Good idea. In the meantime, call for a press conference, so I can deny any part in this."

Bonifield entered Jean's office and stood nervously in front of her desk and waited until she finished talking on the phone. He ran his fingers across her new nameplate on the desk, *Assistant Project Coordinator.* "Is something going on around here I should know about, Jean?"

"Probably best you don't know, Eddy," she answered.

"But all these people rushing in and out and whispering things is very distracting."

"How can you hear anything from inside your office?"

"Holding my ear against a water glass to the door works fairly well. Otherwise I have to leave the door cracked open a bit."

"I guess you're bound to find out sooner or later. The Mars ship is lost."

"It wasn't something I did, was it?"

"I think this is something a little beyond even your sphere of influence, Eddy."

"Then why did you have to tell me?"

"In case anybody asks you about a missing space ship, you can tell them your assistant project coordinator has everything under control, and they should ask her about it."

"Oh. Well, it's a relief to know you have everything under control." He picked up a rubber band off her desk and walked back to his office.

A few minutes later, Dave walked into Jean's office with a small recording machine in his hand. "I believe I found our space ship, Jean."

She leaned back in her chair and asked, "This had better not be a lead-in for one of your corny jokes."

"Real deal," he said as he held up his fingers in the Boy Scout's honor position. "I had the boys in the audio section take out all the interference in the transmission about being lost." Then he grinned. "You're going to get a kick out this."

"I thought you said this wasn't a joke setup."

"It's funny, but not one of my jokes." He turned on the recorder, smiled, and stood back with his arms crossed. "Just listen to this."

After they had listened to the entire recording, Jean tilted her head in a puzzled expression. "I heard it clear enough, but I don't recognize any of those voices. And," she added, "I'm totally confused over that last part."

"Buy me and Eddy lunch for a quick explanation?"

"Oh, what the hell. It's probably my turn anyway."

"The audio guys finally figured out the voices were part of the old TV show, *Lost in Space.*"

"A *television* program?"

"Evidently, somebody on board had a copy of it and played it over the ship's radio by mistake."

Jean leaned forward and said, "Then they're not really lost at all?"

"Nope."

She flopped back in her chair. "Oh, what a relief. But what was all that racket after the voices?"

Dave finally laughed out loud. "Believe it or not, it was an accordion playing the theme from the TV series, *Star Trek.*"

End

MEET THE AUTHOR

Aliens abducted me from a cornfield in Nebraska as a young man, but eventually dropped me off in Texas where I've called home off and on ever since.

Now I'm still off, but a firmly transplanted Texan in Lancaster, just south of Dallas.

Aside from my own writing, I'm also the head writer for Win Shields Productions in Dallas.

I hide behind the email: revup44@gmail.com

COMING SOON

THE MARMER SYSTEM ROGUES

My next book is an action packed science fiction novel, due to come out in the next few months.

A rough and tumble small time thief becomes a space pirate/rogue in a binary star system. Bril's craftiness keeps him alive while dealing with a powerful crime boss, his own violent crew, evading the Interplanetary Police, and bad luck.

While Bril continues his marauding, two small boys are growing up on the planet Stollan and having their own problems. When one becomes a young man and the other a teenager, they join Bril's crew. Along with their problems they bring a promise of great wealth, and Bril wants it for himself.

But more danger and bad luck falls on them all before they reach their final destination.

www.ingramcontent.com/pod-product-compliance
Lightning Source LLC
Chambersburg PA
CBHW061140170626
46809CB00003B/938